Betsy Tobin was born in the Ame[...] [...] England in 1989. She lives in Lond[...] [...] children. *The Bounce* is her second n[...] [...] *Bone House*, is also published by Revie[...] [...] for the Commonwealth Prize (First Novel) and [...]on a Herodotus Prize in America.

Praise for *Bone House*:

'Betsy Tobin['s] . . . debut novel mesmeris[...] the reader with its gentle mysticism, carnal themes and dream-like qualities . . . a fine gothic novel which burrows unde[...] the skin'   *The Times*

'Tobin's mesmeric tale . . . Filled with superstition and desire, murder and medicine, this is a fable with a darkly modern edge'   *Daily Mail*

'A wonderful and moving novel . . . it deserves the widest possible readership'   Iain Pears, author of *An Instance of the Fingerpost*

'Wonderful! . . . a compelling mystery . . . poignant and gripping'   Tracy Chevalier, author of *Girl with a Pearl Earring*

'Tobin's neatly measured prose cuts through a tangle of dark and dirty secrets . . . with pearly clarity . . . Her writing has weight and resonance . . . a compelling story of haunted lives'   *Time Out*

'An entertaining and highly original first novel'   *Harpers and Queen*

'A gripping narrative . . . a tale shimmering with psychological depth'   *New York Times*

Also by Betsy Tobin

Bone House

The Bounce

Betsy Tobin

review

First published in 2002
by REVIEW

An imprint of Headline Book Publishing

First published in paperback in 2003

10 9 8 7 6 5 4 3 2 1

ISBN 0 7472 6496 1

Typeset in Perpetua by
Letterpart Limited, Reigate, Surrey

Printed and bound in Great Britain by
Clays Ltd, St Ives plc

HEADLINE BOOK PUBLISHING
A division of Hodder Headline
338 Euston Road
LONDON NW1 3BH

www.reviewbooks.co.uk
www.hodderheadline.com

For Mickey and Jim with love

He threw himself down on the ground with the Lioness over him; and then half lying down, allowed the Lioness to come behind him, and then pushed his head into her mouth; she also licked his hair (all the time behind him) like a dog would your face . . . It's quite beautiful to see, and makes me wish I could do the same.

Queen Victoria
1838

1

Nathan

I N THE DARKEST hour, he is swimming like a salmon towards his mother. She moves through the water just ahead of him, her long dark hair fanning backwards, beckoning. With a flick of her tail, she shoots forward and disappears, leaving him alone upon the vast ocean swell. He turns and sees the ship's prow looming right in front of him. And in the next instant he is awake, sweating, in his tiny metal berth. He feels the ship roll uneasily beneath him. Two weeks ago he had never seen the ocean. Now he can no longer remember the feel of land beneath his feet.

The next morning, the ship leaves the cold waters of the Atlantic and steams up the long, grey ribbon of the Thames. Nathan stands on the ship's upper deck watching the dark face of London in the distance. For twelve days he has seen nothing but the line of the horizon. Now he sees only endless rows of buildings, made of blackened brick and wood and stone. And the sky is of a colour he would not have dreamed possible. Singed by the smoke of a thousand chimneys, it is a dirty yellow haze.

It takes hours for the ship to berth. Amid much shouting and heaving to, the ship finally succeeds in navigating the crowded waters, the great iron hulls jostling for space along the docks like a colony of giant sea birds. London Bridge rises up in front of him like some colossal beast, so close that he can hear the faint slap of water against its grey stone arches. He can just make out the crowded roofs of omnibuses inching along the parapet. Beyond it, the river heaves with activity. He can see half a dozen densely packed steamers, and scores of tugs and fishing boats and mooring barges darting among the waves. Further along he can see more bridges, so close they appear to be stacked upon each other in an extravagant feat of engineering.

At the last moment, he is afraid to disembark. He hovers on the foredeck, is almost the last to clamber down the gangway. And when his feet first hit the shore, Nathan panics. The air is so dense it stings his eyes and snags in his chest. And he cannot see the sun, though he knows it to be there. He wonders for a moment whether his journey has been wasted, for he cannot imagine that his mother would choose to settle in such a place as this.

He sees at once that London is far too big a place to locate anyone by chance. That first week he walks for miles. He memorises landmarks, studies maps on station walls, knows by instinct that the better districts are not intended for the likes of him. He keeps to the more densely populated areas, spends hours hovering outside shop windows along the Strand, or roaming the narrow alleyways of Southwark, or listening to hawkers on the crowded steps of St Paul's. Twice he ventures deep into the slums and is stunned: so many people packed so tightly together. He did not think that human beings could exist amid such squalor. And yet there is life in them. These people fight and curse and spit like any others.

He keeps his bearings by the river, returning to it frequently. He marvels again at the number of bridges, has never seen so many in one place, and cannot fathom why they've all been built. Within a few days he has memorised all seven: their size and shape and colour and who uses them. For solace he spends hours perched upon their rails, mesmerised by the flow of tide and traffic beneath him.

The Thames has brought him here and in a sense it quickly owns him. It seems to him the river *is* London: swift, chaotic, dangerous, changeable. The bridges themselves are evidence of this: the people here have somehow tried to bind the land and water, have laced it together with stone and iron so it cannot come apart. And though he fears the river's murky currents, Nathan is also drawn to them, for they are his only means of escape. After that first week, perhaps without realising it, he rarely ventures more than half a mile from its banks.

He finds a room in a swampy Lambeth tenement, not as bad as many he's seen, but worse than he is accustomed to. The landlady is a sour-faced widow, and shrewd in her reckoning: ten shillings a week for room and board, payable in advance, and he must furnish his own butter for supper, and candles for lighting to bed. The terms of the arrangement surprise him, and when he finds the cold mutton pie she leaves out for him the first evening, he is dismayed. What little meat there is lurks within a suspiciously dense and odd-coloured gravy, and the heavily larded pastry sticks in his gullet.

After the first week, he decides he must begin searching in earnest for his mother. And so he makes the rounds of music halls and amphitheatres, pleasure gardens and any other places of entertainment he can find. This time he does not wander. He starts with the top establishments of the West End. The Alhambra and the Egyptian Palace, the splendid theatres of the Strand – the sort of places he has always imagined her to be in. He is disappointed when he does not find her, but not deterred. He travels on to the East End, to the penny theatres and music halls of Bethnal Green and Whitechapel. More than once he is taken aback by the rude acts and rough clientele. He tells himself that he will not find his mother in such places, but each time he still enquires. Finally, he heads south of the river, to the pleasure halls of Southwark and Lambeth.

He carries her picture with him always, the faded playbill he discovered as a child. In it she is pictured astride a white stallion, the horse's reins drawn up sharply in her hands, her long dark hair falling in a tangle of curls, her expression triumphant. Everywhere he ventures Nathan shows it, carefully unfolding the yellowed paper, pointing to the creased image of the woman who was once his mother. He hates this act of sharing her with strangers, bearded men with jaundiced eyes and hacking coughs, theatre managers, music-hall owners, circus proprietors, booking agents. One by one they shake their heads and narrow their gaze at him, as if by searching for her he somehow demeans himself. We should not admit to this, he thinks one night as he walks slowly back along the Embankment, to the need for one another.

Little by little, the urgency of his quest slackens. He takes to rising late in the morning, and wanders out into the street at midday, his mind hazy from oversleep. He can think of no other means of searching. He buys a map of Europe, wondering whether his mother has not escaped to some other place – Paris, Berlin, Vienna. Nathan stares down at the rash of small red circles with dismay. His mother could be anywhere inside them.

2

The Lions

QUEEN IS DREAMING. She is running fast on the veldt, the scent of buffalo exploding in her nostrils. She threads her way through a dense grove of young acacia, and emerges out into a clearing, where she stops short. She is eager to find the herd, but something in the lay of the grass ahead makes her pause. It is a dark, moonless night and the ground in front of her is thickly strewn with new-cut brush, as if a herd of elephants has just swept through. But the scattered tangle of boughs strikes her oddly. She listens intently for a few moments, then turns and begins gingerly to retrace her steps. As she does, she hears a noise not far in front of her, from the direction she has come. It is a sound she has never heard before – the whisper-soft click of metal – and it is enough to make the hair along her spine bristle. Once again she pauses, her entire body taut with concentration. She listens for a moment, then changes direction a second time. She heads back towards the clearing and breaks into a lope. She aims to lose herself in the thick undergrowth on the other side, but in an instant the boughs give way beneath her feet, and she is falling fast.

Queen lands heavily in the dirt, and hears a chorus of noise from above. The sound is unfamiliar, a little like the jabbering of baboons, only less shrill. She looks around her, stunned. The hole is deep, more than twice her height. She hears a rustling from above and, after a moment, sees a row of wagging faces peering down at her. Queen crouches low and squints up at them: black eyes, brown flesh, white teeth, their tiny heads wrapped in cloth. In that moment, she feels the sickening punch of regret.

They cast their nets upon her. She struggles against them, but the fibres snag upon her teeth and claws, and before long she is so well trussed that she can hardly move. The men wave their arms excitedly, and after a series of shouts, they slowly raise her from the depths of the hole. She sees them strain against her weight, sees how small and thin they are compared to her. They carry her a short distance, then drop her heavily on her side upon the ground. She lies in the long grass, panting with fear. The men peer at her from a distance, and one takes a long stick and prods her belly with it. She twists round and snarls at him, and his companions burst into laughter. Queen stares at them and wishes she were dead.

One man remains behind to watch her. He is smaller than the others, and she thinks how easily she could crush his skull with one quick blow of her paw. She watches in horror as he builds a fire, and within a few minutes the smell of wood smoke clogs her nostrils. The night passes slowly. Although the man dozes briefly, Queen does not. She is relieved when the flames die away and the first rays of dawn appear. Before long she hears voices from the bush, and the others return. They sling the ends of the net across a long wooden pole, and she feels herself being lifted once again into the air. The weight of her body strains uncomfortably against the coarse mesh of the net. The men walk in a long line across the veldt, and the constant swaying of the net makes her dizzy. As the sun rises high into the sky, Queen closes her eyes and tries to forget herself.

3

Nathan

NATHAN HAS COME to see a booking agent near Vauxhall Station. The office is up a narrow flight of stairs behind a run-down gin palace, and as he climbs the steps he can hear shouts of drunken laughter from below. The floor is dirty and unswept, and the walls along the corridor are stained a dingy brown, but when he reaches the office door he can see that it is freshly painted. A small wooden sign on it reads: 'Joseph Stickley, Theatrical Agent'. Nathan knocks and opens the door a crack to find a large man with beefy cheeks staring at him from behind a massive wooden desk. He is nearly bald, except for an arc of fuzzy grey hair above each ear, and his beard is neatly trimmed. An unlit cigar dangles loosely from the corner of his lips, and his bulging eyes are hung with dark circles.

Nathan stammers out his purpose, his hands shaking as he withdraws the folded playbill once again from the pocket of his coat. At the sight of it the man takes the cigar from the side of his mouth and peers at him.

'This is more than ten years old, lad.'

'Yes, sir,' he says.

'She's finished with performing.'

Nathan frowns; this had not occurred to him.

Stickley leans forward, his chair creaking. 'What's your business with her?' he asks.

Nathan hesitates. 'She owes me something,' he says finally. A life, he thinks.

Stickley shoves the cigar behind one ear and opens a leather-bound ledger on the desk in front of him. 'She's got an interest in a show not far from here. Owns it jointly with an associate of mine, though she doesn't have much to do with it. He runs it and I handle the bookings.' He looks up. 'Is it a job you're after?'

Nathan considers this. 'Could be.'

'You work the shows?'

'All my life.'

Stickley looks at him askance. 'Not *here*,' he says sceptically.

'No, sir. I worked the mud circus – St Louis, Minneapolis, Twin Rivers, Great Falls. And every town in between.'

Stickley raises his eyebrows and grunts. 'Can you ride?' he asks.

'I can sit a horse, if that's what you mean.'

'Stunt riding.'

'No, sir.' She never taught me, he thinks. She could have taught me at least that. Though in truth, he has never liked horses.

'You walk the rope or work the bars?'

'No, sir . . .' Nathan's voice tails off with embarrassment.

'Well, what *do* you do?'

'Strike the show, drive the teams. Advance billing, scout work.'

Stickley laughs and shakes his head. 'None of that here, lad! This is London: the people come to us. Unless of course you've a mind to go out on the road, tour the fairs and market towns and such. But you'll have to wait for spring, the season's over. And anyway, that's not my game.' He slams the ledger shut with a thud. Nathan watches as he jams the cigar between his fleshy lips and strikes a match, puffing deeply several times.

'I'm good with animals,' Nathan says finally.

The big man looks up at him, then reopens the ledger and scans it. 'I could use a cage boy,' he says slowly.

Nathan looks at him blankly.

'Big cats, boy. Lions. That's all the people want to see.'

Nathan thinks of the menagerie he used to run: a cow with two udders, an ostrich, a three-legged coyote, and a pig that could balance an apple on the tip of its snout. 'I could do that,' he says evenly. He has never seen a lion.

Stickley squints at him, measuring his worth. 'The wages aren't much,' he says briskly.

Nathan shrugs. 'Don't mind. As long as it'll keep me.'

'Oh, it'll keep you. After a fashion.' He hands Nathan a small white card. 'The man you want is Talliot. You'll find him just off Lambeth Walk. Tell him you're the new cage boy.'

Nathan reaches out and takes the card. He nods towards the playbill.

'Will *she* be there?'

Stickley pauses, eyeing him. 'I'd stay clear of her if I was you.'

4

Lulu

L ULU THE ROPE dancer, freshly perfumed and
painted, waits for his cue from behind the velvet
curtain. Just beyond the fabric he can see the
newcomer crouching on his haunches, his face like an angel's.
The boy's skin glows pink in the light of the gas lamps, and
his dark eyes shimmer with excitement as he trains his gaze
upon the ring. He turns his head and glimpses Lulu in the
wings, and the look of awe upon his face is one that Lulu
would like to freeze and keep for ever. Lulu winks shame-
lessly and the boy blinks in amazement. After a split second's
hesitation he looks away.

Lulu hears his cue and straightens instantly. He lifts his
chin, moistens his painted lips, fills his chest with air, and
fixes his eyes on a point straight ahead. He sweeps past the
curtain and runs gracefully to the far side of the ring, where
he shimmies quickly up a dangling rope to the platform
overhead. Once aloft he forgets the newcomer, concentrates
only on being her: the divine Lulu. This is what he loves the

most: the audience spread beneath him like a plush carpet of admiration. He scans the waiting throng, relishes their breathless anticipation. The women regard him with fear and envy and something akin to shock, for his flesh-coloured tights and low-cut bustier have been the subject of much speculation this season. The men loosen their cravats and lean forward eagerly, take in every contour, feast upon him with their eyes. Just to see him is worth the price of admission.

For he is Lulu, girl acrobat of their dreams, and he has made himself beautiful for them. It takes him nearly two hours each evening to prepare himself, a labour of love that he willingly endures. Indeed, he revels in it: the powder and rouge and scarlet lip paint; the long tress of golden curls, which he sweeps back in a diamanté clasp and allows to cascade down his back. His figure is finely shaped and he shows it to its best advantage, the scantily cut bloomers artfully concealing those things he'd prefer remain hidden. He waves a naked arm to them just now, then signals to the stagehand opposite, and in an instant he is airborne, his lithe body arcing through the air.

Once in the air he forgets himself completely, thinks only of distance and space and the wooden bar clenched tightly in his hands. He loves the moment of release, when for an instant he defies gravity, suspended in time above the onlookers' heads. In that moment the world outside ceases to exist. He can live a lifetime or not at all, according to his whim. And then he turns and feels the polished wood beneath his fingers once again, and the weight of his body as it swings across the space. He goes through the motions of his routine, six or seven minutes at most, and at the finish every muscle in his frame pulses with exertion, and his powdered brow is beaded with sweat. He ends with a flourish atop the platform, turns and waves to the adoring crowd, which has risen to its feet in a fit of excitement. There is nothing to rival this, he thinks. No equal pleasure – except perhaps a lover's first kiss.

As he dismounts, he sees the boy again, his cheeks two spots of flame. What is it that sets this handsome boy on fire? The thought delights him, and he gives the boy his most coquettish smile as he passes him in the wings, aware suddenly of his own aroma, of perfume mixed with sweat. The audience shouts and stamps and clamours for more, and Lulu turns and passes the boy again, running out into the centre of the ring, where a shower of long-stemmed roses lands at his feet. He blows the audience a kiss, then signals to the orange girl waiting patiently to one side. As always, she smiles and tosses him an orange. He catches it with ease in one hand, holds it aloft and waves it like a flag for the audience to see. Then he brings it to his lips, inhales deeply the smell of citrus, a scent he cherishes, for it reminds him of the lemon groves of his homeland. He blows a final kiss to the crowd, then disappears behind the velvet curtain for the last time.

Quickly he ducks inside the tiny commode that serves as his private dressing room, stripping off the flesh-coloured tights, the satin bodysuit and bloomers. He pulls on magenta-coloured breeches of softest corduroy, the knees so tight he can hardly get them past his muscular calves, and a long olive frock coat with fake mother-of-pearl buttons the size of marbles. He takes pains to remove his make-up, leaving only the faintest trace of red upon his lips, and folds and stores the wig carefully, deep within his bag, as it is human hair and cost him nearly three weeks' wages. Once outside, he must take care not to be recognised. Only last week, a reporter managed to find his way backstage, intent on discovering his well-guarded secret. The man was found and ejected by the manager only seconds before Lulu emerged from the commode.

This time, when he exits, he slams the door to the dressing room more loudly than he should. The cage boy, still crouched in the wings, turns and at once takes in the sight of him. A look of confusion crosses his face, followed perhaps by one of disappointment. Lulu smiles coyly and raises a finger to his lips, never once releasing the boy's gaze from his own. Then he strolls past and steals quietly out by the rear entrance, leaving the boy wide-eyed behind him.

5

The Lions

NERO IS SLEEPING in his favourite pose, his back nestled firmly against the bars of the cage. He lies on his side, legs outstretched, paws turned in. It is an uneasy sleep, and his flesh jumps from time to time. As always, he dreams of long-legged animals, unsuspecting prey, the thrill of the chase. In sleep he is free again, feeling the long grass of the veldt brush against his underside, the hot sun beating down upon his muscular back. He spies a herd of impala grazing near a waterhole in the distance, and breaks into a trot, slowing only when he has closed the gap to little more than a sprint. He crouches low, scanning the herd for the smallest and weakest. Just then a hyena coughs in the distance, breaking his concentration and alerting the herd. Nero raises his head, irritated, and as he does the impala sense danger and begin to stir. In seconds, they are bounding away. He watches helplessly as they disappear against the horizon, and when they are gone he sinks down on to his empty belly in the grass.

Queen, too, is hungry. She paces the bars, awaiting her food, for the tamer is late again. It is already dark outside. The pair of gas lamps suspended on the wall beyond the cage spit and flare noisily. Queen eyes them uneasily each time she turns, the harsh white of their flame a constant source of annoyance to her: she has grown used to their sound and smell but will never settle with the flame. Just then she hears the tamer coming, and as she turns she sees not one but two men approaching the cage.

In a second Nero is awake and on his feet, the scent of horseflesh in his nostrils. He moves past Queen, brushing by her body with his own, asserting the authority of his sex. Queen tolerates him, but it is she who rules the cage and Nero knows it. They continue to pace impatiently as the tamer fumbles with his ring of iron keys. Once again his scent is overpowering, and finding the keys takes an eternity. Queen watches as he sways slightly, grabbing hold of an iron bar to steady himself. She has never seen the boy beside him, but the last one stayed for only three weeks, until he strayed too near the bars and Queen caught him with a claw. That boy had screamed and clutched his arm as the blood began to run, and Queen had seen the whites of his eyes.

The new boy carries the iron tub that holds their meal, thirty pounds of freshly butchered horse meat. He wears a startled look, much like the last one, though something in his bearing suggests that he is fitter for the job. The tamer finally succeeds in unlocking the cage, and before he opens it he

turns to the boy and motions for him to follow. The boy
nods, his face rigid, and the tamer opens the cage door
slowly, brandishing his whip. Nero retreats immediately to
the far side of the cage, but Queen stays where she is, lashing
her tail slowly from side to side. The tamer takes a few steps
towards her, and when she refuses to retreat he raises the
whip and brings it down hard against the floor, causing the
boy to flinch. Queen lowers her ears and snarls, holding her
ground. Behind her Nero crouches low, mindful of the whip.
Queen does not fear the lash as Nero does; has learned to
tolerate its sting.

The tamer instructs the boy to deposit the iron tub at his
feet. The meat is in great hunks and must be divided evenly
between the two, or fighting will ensue. The tamer crouches
down and reaches for a piece, never once taking his eyes off
Queen. He lifts a mass of bloody flesh and bone and hurls it
at Nero in the corner, then reaches back into the tub for
Queen's portion as Nero eagerly pounces on his, sinking his
teeth deep inside. He fumbles with Queen's piece and nearly
drops it, and as he dips his eyes she bounds towards him in a
lightning-fast blur of movement. The tamer jumps backwards, nearly knocking the boy over, and brings the whip
down hard in Queen's direction. Its tip just catches her nose,
for she has been careful not to spring too close, and she
immediately retreats to the far side of the cage. The tamer
swears at her and rights himself, kicking the iron tub at his
feet. Queen sees the boy behind him blanch. She feels the
blood bead up upon her nostril, and the boy's eyes upon her.
The trainer angrily hurls the remainder of the meat in their
direction, then backs hurriedly out of the cage, shouting at

the boy to follow. The boy hesitates, unable to tear his eyes from the sight of Queen devouring her meat, and the tamer swears at him. Queen raises her head to stare at the boy, and the two of them lock eyes. His scent is different, unlike any she has ever known.

6

Nathan

EACH MORNING HE walks to work a little breathless with anticipation, his insides roiling at the prospect that his mother will be there. But each day he is at first disappointed, and then relieved. Nathan does not know if he will have the courage to confront her. When he imagines a meeting, the words fly from his head like startled birds, leaving him mute.

A week after joining the circus, he wakes one morning from a heavy, dreamless sleep. The sky outside his window is tobacco brown, and he can hear a gust of wind rattle the glass. He rolls over and closes his eyes. For the first time, the very thought of London overwhelms him. Perhaps he has been wrong to come. Perhaps he should abandon the search for his mother, even though he is so close. He has a little money left, enough to buy a passage somewhere. But he can think of nowhere he would go.

And he has the animals to consider. He is now in charge of the entire menagerie. Nathan does not flatter himself, for he can see it is a job no one wants. The animals are a forlorn assortment: Nero and Queen occupy the centre cage in the menagerie tent and are the main lure for the audience, who are charged an additional penny to enter the tent before or after the main show. An ageing orang-utan called Kezia has a small cage to herself in one corner, and although the cage is fitted with dangling ropes and a wooden swing, she spends most of her time hiding in a large wooden crate filled with straw. In the opposite corner stands a tall mesh cage containing two parakeets and a toucan. They seem to Nathan the happiest of the lot, partly because they are the noisiest, and partly because it is impossible to read anything in their beady expressions. The last cage is occupied by a six-foot boa constrictor who rarely budges, except during its weekly feeding, when it moves surprisingly quickly. This occurs on Saturday nights and Talliot makes a special show of the event, dangling two large rats by the tail before dropping them into the cage, and charging twice the entrance fee.

In addition to the animals, the menagerie tent also boasts a bar and a freak act. The bar is long and handsome, made of polished oak and fine brass fitments that sparkle in the gaslight. It sells ginger beer, brandy and individual mutton pies, and is tended by a retired performer called Walter Simms. The old man lost an arm just below the shoulder in an accident many years ago. This itself is a curiosity, and he is often asked by punters to raise his dangling shirtsleeve to reveal the reddened stump hidden underneath. Nathan, too, stared at it the first time, taken aback by the sight of scarred flesh and grizzled muscle. The old man does not object to the display, indeed he appears to relish it, encouraging the bravest of the patrons to touch the stump if they dare. Nathan recognises something in the old man that he has seen all his life: this need to amplify oneself. And while he himself has been born and bred among performers, he knows that he is missing this sense of showmanship, much as the old man lacks a limb.

The final occupant of the menagerie tent is not an animal but a man. The Skeleton Man is advertised on the handbill as a fully grown man of nearly six feet in height who weighs only fifty-nine pounds. His name is Karl Grossinger and he stands quietly by the bar or sometimes perches delicately upon a stool. He speaks very little and smiles even less, and it is some days before Nathan summons the courage to meet his gaze, which is surprisingly strong and clear. He is exceedingly thin in the face and arms, and his shoulders are rounded forward beneath his baggy coat, but otherwise he appears almost normal. He has lost most of his hair, and that which remains has turned a dull grey despite his relative youth, for according to the handbill he is only thirty-four years of age. Each night Nathan watches as his wife and three young children come to collect him after the show, because he finds it difficult to walk without the aid of an escort. His wife is a sturdy young woman with a plain face and a serious expression, who wears her obvious poverty with quiet dignity. She carries an infant girl strapped to her back so as to keep her hands free to assist her husband, and Nathan cannot help but notice the dimples in the baby's ruddy cheeks as it bobs along upon its mother's back. The oldest child, a boy of eight or nine, holds the hand of his younger brother, and the two walk slowly behind their parents. Carl's wife wraps a thick knitted scarf around his neck before they face the November winds. Nathan feels a pang of longing each time he observes her brushing aside a stray wisp of hair from his eyes. Once he sees Carl stumble and fall just outside the tent, and all three of them, the sturdy young woman and her two sons, immediately bend to help him to his feet. They achieve this with some difficulty, a look of anguish on their faces, and when Carl is finally righted they stand, the four of them, holding each other in a tight circle. From just inside the tent Nathan watches as the baby girl twists her head round to catch a glimpse of her family, aware somehow that she is on the outside of something desirable.

Gradually, Nathan comes to know the lions and their tamer. The latter is a short, sullen man in his early forties, with a large moustache, and a thick head of dark hair, which he oils and combs straight back before each performance. He has a long scar that stretches from his left ear down the length of his neck, disappearing beneath his collar, and he often raises his fingertips to it without realising. According to Walter he was wounded by a tigress some years before, and as a consequence has sworn never to enter a cage with that breed again. More often than not he is drunk by showtime, and twice Walter has been forced to sit him down with a steaming cup of coffee to sober him before the performance.

The lions hate him. Even Nathan can see that, for when the tamer enters the cage they flatten their ears and narrow their eyes, lashing their tails anxiously from side to side. Night after night Nathan watches from the wings as the tamer lurches through his act, his bloodshot eyes wild with fear. And although Nathan knows nothing of these animals, his instinct tells him that this man debases them all with his cracking whip and angry shouts and too-florid complexion. The lions grudgingly go through their paces like a pair of insolent teenagers, leaping upon the pedestals, sitting on their haunches and roaring in unison. Most nights the tamer whips them into a frenzy of anger, makes them leap about the cage in a display of such ferocity that it is a wonder they do not turn and shred him to pieces.

Nathan watches the crowd's response, for it is not just the lions who are whipped into a frenzy. The wilder the act, the more the crowd hoots and bays its appreciation, jumping to its feet and stamping on the wooden benches. The sight makes him uneasy. One night, while he is watching, he turns and sees the Skeleton Man just behind him in the darkness, his disquieting gaze trained upon the lions. When the act is finished and the tamer has emerged, sweaty and triumphant, from the cage, the Skeleton Man speaks to him in quiet tones, his voice cutting through the thunderous applause like a steel blade. 'How ridiculous human excitement is,' he says. And then without another word he turns away, and with his peculiar shuffling gait disappears behind the velvet curtain. Nathan stands in stunned silence after he goes, for it is the first time the Skeleton Man has ever spoken to him.

He spends most of each evening in the menagerie tent, except during the lion act when he is required to hover in the wings in case the tamer signals for assistance. He sees the show in its entirety the first night, forcing himself to sit through even the equestrian act, though the sight of horses in the ring sickens him. He has carried this aversion with him as long as he can remember, ever since as a tiny child, he was made to watch his mother perform, the fear trapped inside him. His memories of her astride a horse are still vivid, even though he can no longer conjure up the image of her face. But he can see the flesh of her thighs wrapped around the horse's wide girth, and the muscles of her back straining as she leans forward into its neck.

Nathan can rarely resist the lure of Lulu, though he makes a point of hiding deep within the crowd. He is drawn to him in spite of himself, for the desire which rises up in him when Lulu enters the ring each evening fills him with shame. Were Lulu a woman, Nathan would not fight his attraction, but the knowledge of Lulu's sex is like a coiled snake of conscience, ready to strike at any moment. Try as he might, he cannot reconcile himself to it. Another man might shrug his shoulders and allow himself the luxury of the moment, but Nathan is unable to do so. Instead he torments himself each night with the sight of him, memorising every detail of his perfectly formed limbs, the curve of his slender waist, the arch of his dark eyebrows, the lush crimson of his lips. He hates himself for it.

One night shortly after his arrival, Lulu comes to the menagerie tent after his performance. He sits at the bar, still fully made up in the blond hairpiece and satin bloomers, daintily sipping a sherry. He chats idly with Walter while the Skeleton Man looks on and Nathan busies himself with the cages. Lulu allows his gaze to follow Nathan about the tent, and once he even chances a casual remark as he passes by, but Nathan lowers his eyes and pretends not to hear. He is disconcerted by the sound of Lulu's voice, for it is not as low as he imagined it would be; indeed it could easily pass for a woman's. Lulu speaks English fluently but not without an accent, a fact that makes him seem even more alluring in Nathan's eyes. In the end he is saved by Talliot, who enters just before the show's finale and insists Lulu leave at once, before the tent fills up with patrons. Lulu jumps lightly from the stool and looks Talliot directly in the eye, before turning on his heel and leaving, and Nathan sees at once the animosity between them. Talliot stands for a moment after the rope dancer has gone, his fists clenched at his sides, and Nathan sees his gaze come to rest on Lulu's sherry glass, with its perfect crimson stain.

At night he dreams as usual of his mother in the ring, only now her face and body are those of Lulu, for it is Lulu's thighs that grip the horse's middle, and Lulu's lips that form a knowing smile each time he comes round the ring. He cannot see himself in these dreams, cannot divine whether he is a child of three or a young man of nineteen. He knows only the rapid beat of his heart and the throbbing dampness in his groin when he awakes. The dreams humiliate him and he bears the shame of them like a great weight, convinced his guilt is evident for all to see. For this reason he keeps largely to himself.

7

Nan

NAN STANDS FROZEN in the wings, watching Lulu soar like a starling overhead. Nothing matters to her: not the pull of fruit upon her neck, nor the oily leer of those who want more than oranges for their money. Lulu's life is the stuff of dreams, and when he flies through the air, for a moment she forgets her own. Now she watches as he climbs up the rope and grabs the bar. In her hand is an orange, and when Lulu's feet leave the platform, she gives the fruit a little squeeze of encouragement. She always chooses the biggest and sweetest-smelling orange in her basket, as if it is a measure of her worth. When Lulu's hands leave the bar, Nan shuts her eyes and spreads her wings. Now it is Nan who flies, her hand still tight upon the orange. Nan and her orange are soaring, away from this wretched land for ever.

The crowd trills. Nan opens her eyes and Lulu stands on the platform, waving. Now he is no longer a starling, but an angel of grace and deception. She watches as he returns to earth, sees him skip about the ring with delight. The crowd is bursting now. It jumps to its feet and surges forward en masse. Those at the back strain to catch a glimpse of the dainty beads of sweat that have formed on Lulu's upper lip. Now that Lulu is on the ground, Nan can almost reach out and tweak the crowd's desire. The flowers start to fall: long-stemmed roses of red and pink and white. Lulu skitters to and fro, gathering them in his arms, stopping now and then to smell their scent.

Nan turns away, ashamed of the envy that hoodwinks her each night. She owes her livelihood to Lulu, and her independence. Lulu used his influence with the crippled woman, and now Nan is the only one allowed to sell inside the tent. The others must wait outside and try their luck. They hate her for it but she doesn't mind. Inside the tent her living is secure. Without the others she can charge a higher price. Spectacle makes them hungry, and desire makes them lose their sense. Now she sells three times as many oranges as before, and does not have to walk the streets from dawn to dusk.

Nan watches the crowd. She spies the handsome cage boy tucked discreetly in the back, and cranes to get a better view. She can see the dark look of desire on his face. So he *is* a man after all, she thinks. For a moment she allows her eyes to linger on him, this strange American lad who rarely utters a word and never meets her gaze. He goes about his work with such earnest dedication that she thought perhaps it was the animals he fancied. But of course it is Lulu.

She cannot tear her eyes from him. How unlike other men he seems. The skin on his face is smooth and hairless, and his cheeks are pink, like a baby's. Maybe that is why she looks at him, though he is shy and never meets her gaze. Perhaps all men from America are strange like him. They say it is a place of excess, where people come and go just as they please. Not like here, thinks Nan, where if you're born in the muck, it sticks to you and you to it. But she should not look at him, for she does not trust herself with men. She'll not set up with one again.

Nan turns back to the ring just in time, for she has nearly missed Lulu's signal. The orange is ready in her hand. She tosses it in a perfect arc across the ring to where he stands. At that instant, she feels the crowd's desire swivel towards her like the barrel of a loaded gun. Now it is Nan they watch. She feels the flush rise in her cheeks, the quickening of her pulse. She smiles at them, the way Lulu does. But it does not come as easily to her.

Lulu takes his final bow and disappears behind the curtain. Two stagehands appear and begin to set up props for the next act. The band starts to play. The crowd shifts restlessly. Almost at once, a knot of eager young men appears in front of Nan, as if it is a piece of Lulu they are buying, and not just fruit. She serves them as quickly as she can, and for the next few minutes she is kept busy selling the remainder of her stock. When the basket is empty, Nan raises her eyes to find the handsome cage boy in the crowd, but he is gone.

8
Lulu

BACK IN HIS dressing room, Lulu relishes the first spurt of citrus upon his tongue. Performance makes him thirsty, and he devours half a dozen oranges every night to replenish his strength. Nan leaves them for him in his tiny room, even peels them in advance: a token of her gratitude. She owes her full purse each evening to him, but it is not her only debt, for it is Lulu who found her in a narrow street behind Drury Lane in the middle of the night, clutching her dead infant in her arms.

The first time they meet, he comes upon her quite by accident. He is hurrying to a nightclub and has paused for a moment beneath the flare of a gas lamp to check the time. He hears a cough in the darkness, and when he looks up he sees her standing in the shadows, her eyes locked on his. He has the curious sensation that she is awaiting him. He walks slowly to where she stands, clutching a small bundle tightly to her chest. He stops just in front of her and, when he looks into her eyes, he recognises himself in them. He looks down at the face of the child, and realises with a start that it is dead.

After a moment's hesitation, she allows him to pry the baby's body from her grasp. It has begun to rain lightly, and the threadbare blanket that serves as a shroud is damp.

He sees that she is half-frozen. Holding the infant tightly with one arm, he leads her by the hand through the darkened streets to a chophouse in Leicester Square, the only establishment he can find that is open. The girl's lips are blue with cold, or maybe it is with grief, but her expression is strangely luminous, as if it is she who's just ascended to heaven, not the child. At first she cannot eat, merely stares at the slab of beef on her plate. But eventually she devours three full plates of food, much to the amazement of the boy who serves them. Lulu orders her brandy and coffee at the end, and she holds it tightly between the palms of her hands. Not once during the meal does she venture a glance under the table, where the infant is lodged upon his lap.

He has a friend who is a priest, he tells her. A good friend who will give the child a proper burial. She nods slowly, seeming relieved by this, though in truth he does not know a priest, only a choirboy whom he has corrupted. But he knows that he can help her; indeed, he feels an overwhelming compulsion to do so, as if they've been dropped together on this earth like two flakes of snow.

Eventually her story spills out and, although whole oceans separate their birth, he decides later that their lives are not so very different. The girl has spent most of her life in London, though her people have come from Ireland. Even as a tiny child, she tells him, she had the sense of being lost among her own. She is neither English nor Irish, and when she tries to root herself in either culture nothing grows. The baby is proof of this, she says. His birth was blighted from the start, for the wee thing refused to suckle and wasted away before her very eyes, despite her increasingly frantic efforts to dribble life into its tiny mouth from a spoon.

She had eight weeks with the child before it finally succumbed. In the last few hours, she cradled him as tightly as she dared, as if she could somehow stop his passing through sheer force of will. The boy's father was struck dumb by his death. He was a young dockhand she'd known since childhood, though by the time the baby was born, the affair had soured. Perhaps she'd confused familiarity with love. The love she experienced for her son was as fierce and painful as a wound. Now she can't give a name to what she'd felt for his father.

However, for reasons she does not fully understand, the boy's father will not let her go. This perplexes and angers her, for surely love is not a token to be passed from one hand to another, but something to be held in unison. The boy's father seemed to sense her withdrawal. The more she turned from him, the more demanding he became, until finally she was forced to bar the door against him. Even then he lurked near her room and, when the baby finally died, he broke down in despair, until she had to bring him in and lay his head upon her lap, the dead child still clasped tightly against her shoulder.

Eventually he fell asleep, and she crept out from under him, fleeing the room with the child swaddled tightly in a blanket. Her first thought was to find a graveyard, where she could bury the boy herself in secret. But when she arrived, she was appalled by the overcrowding and the squalor, for the dead were piled on top of one another in barely covered graves. She wandered for several hours until she could walk no further, stopping finally in a back street in Covent Garden. She does not know how long she had been there when Lulu found her, nor why she chose that particular place to pause. Dozens of people must have passed, their arms laden with purchases, their heads filled with visions of the evening ahead. As the evening progressed, there were fewer passers-by, until night finally fell and she and the child were left alone.

Lulu listens silently as she tells her tale. The dead boy lies upon his thighs like a tightly wrapped burden, and he keeps one hand discreetly upon its middle to prevent it sliding to the floor. He is mesmerised by the rise and fall of the girl's voice, and by her looks, for once inside the chophouse he can see that beneath all the hardship she is far from plain. Her eyes are large and dark and round, with heavy brows as thick as caterpillars. Her face is narrow and heart-shaped, with a long nose and a mouth that was small but beautifully shaped. Her hair is dark as well, and falls in unruly waves below her shoulders, for she wears no covering upon her head. Her skin is smooth and pale, and she is thin to the point of gauntness, but that only serves to sharpen her features. Overall there is a starkness to her that almost frightens him. It is the sort of beauty that cannot be enhanced with powder and paint like his own, and he envies her for it, though she appears unaware.

When she finishes her food, he brings her with him to his lodgings and insists she sleep in his bed, while he makes do with the floor. She looks at him closely, seems to fathom his inclinations, and smiles her gratitude before falling quickly into sleep. He lies on his makeshift bed and dozes fitfully, dreaming of the girl's angular face. In the morning he offers to accompany her to church, as she wishes to say a prayer for her dead son's soul. They kneel side by side in the crowded pew, the scent of evergreen and candle smoke and incense all around them.

9

Nathan

AT NIGHT HE sits alone upon his bed, fingering the tooled leather volume he purchased from a shop on the Strand. It is the first book he has ever owned, and he handles it gingerly, as if the words themselves might break. The spine of the book is bound in dark brown leather, and the cover is marbled with swirls of black and brown and burgundy. Inside, the book is thickly studded with black and white engravings, their intricately shaded renderings like tiny works of art. Less frequently, a richly coloured illustration rises up from the pages like the iridescent plumage of a peacock. In the dingy half-light of a candle, Nathan believes the book to be an object of perfect beauty.

He had seen the shop many times, had lingered more than once outside its bowed glass window. One day the shop's proprietor caught his gaze, and Nathan felt compelled to enter. Inside was a long narrow room, crammed from floor to ceiling with books of every size and description. The air was heavy with the smell of ink, and Nathan saw at once that he was the only customer. The shop's proprietor waited for him to speak, and on a sudden impulse, Nathan asked for a book on animals. The man frowned at him, as if the request was somehow irksome, and then he limped slowly to the back of the shop. He was a small bearded man, well advanced in age, and Nathan could not help but notice an air of disappointment about him, as if the books themselves had somehow let him down. He returned a few moments later with a densely printed scientific volume entitled simply *Zoologica*. Nathan opened the book and stared at the tiny print while the shopkeeper looked on. Though he'd learned his letters as a child, the book was written in a language that stretched far beyond him. He blushed, feeling sure that his lack of learning must somehow be evident, like the man's crippled leg. After a moment, he closed the book and handed it to the owner with an embarrassed shake of his head.

The man took the volume and returned it to the shelf with a little sigh, as if he'd known it would not be purchased in the first place. Nathan turned to go and was nearly out the door when the older man stopped him with a shout. This time he limped more quickly to the front of the shop, clutching in his hand the marbled brown volume. Hesitantly, Nathan took the book from him and opened the cover. His heart sank when he read the title: *Wild Sports of the World*. It was a book about trophy hunting, the very notion of which repelled him. But opposite the title was a neatly folded page of thin paper. Nathan carefully unfolded it and saw that it was a map of Africa. The map was drawn in delicate spidery lines, and dotted across the continent were the tiny figures of wild animals. He peered intently at them, and knew at once by the rushing of his pulse that he would buy the book.

It cost him a guinea, nearly a week's earnings. Even now he does not regret it. Aside from the lions, the book is his only companion. When he is not working, he returns to the dingy room he rents and stretches out on the bed, quickly losing himself among its pages. At times he reads the text, but mainly he prefers to linger over the illustrations. His favourite shows a hunter being tossed high into the air by a bull elephant. The hunter's rifle flies like kindling from his hands. The elephant's trunk is wrapped tightly round the hunter's chest like a tourniquet, and the man's body hangs limply, as if the life has already been squeezed out of him. Blood is splattered across the elephant's trunk and tusks, but the enraged animal is unaware. The picture enthrals Nathan.

One night he reads with horror of the Roman emperor Claudius, who ordered the capture of eleven thousand wild animals for sport. During the course of one week, more than five hundred lions were slain in hand-to-hand combat with slaves. Reading the passage, it does not occur to Nathan to consider the plight of the slaves. He can think only of the fear and bewilderment of the newly captured lions when faced with the sight of thousands screaming for their blood. But then he remembers the life Queen and Nero lead. He thinks of iron bars and butchered meat and the baying of the audience. The thought unsettles him, and he shuts the book's marbled cover with a dull thud. Nathan lies back upon his bed and closes his eyes, but still he hears the clamour of the crowd.

10

Nan

AT NIGHT, IF she tries hard enough, she can feel the milk of his baby breath upon her face. It was sweet and warm and shallow, and at times he'd had to fight for it. There were moments when his breathing had seemed to cease altogether, causing her heart to race with terror. He had died a thousand deaths that way, before the last.

She had memorised his body. The tiny blister on his upper lip, the snail-like curl of his ears, the snip of moon upon his fingertips. Now, when she shuts her eyes, what she sees is the set of his tiny face in sleep: mouth puckered, cheeks at rest, dark eyelashes unfurled against his skin.

The boy's birth had buoyed her. She had not anticipated how much his life would transform her own. Here at last, some small piece of luck had come to her. She was fiercely protective and guarded him closely, lest some harm should befall him. Late at night, she would hold him tightly and conjure a future for them both out of the darkness.

Occasionally, the long shadow of her childhood would steal upon her. At such times she could not help but wonder what her own birth had engendered. The thought saddened her. As a child, she had closed her eyes to the steady, downward spiral of her mother's life. She tried not to dwell on what went wrong, as if the fact of her past might somehow poison her future, and that of her child.

11

Nathan

NATHAN IS IN the cage again. But this time he is alone, and it is as if he is meeting Queen and Nero for the first time. An hour earlier he looked for the tamer and found him sprawled across the floor of his room, his trousers unbuttoned, a dark stain upon his crotch. The room stank of booze and urine. It is worse than the acrid reek of animals, he thought. This man *is* an animal. Now Nathan must exercise the lions himself, because if he leaves them they will be agitated during their evening performance, excitable and dangerous. It is his first time alone with them, and the whip feels heavy in his hand: ill-suited to his grip. However, he has seen the tamer with them so many times he knows precisely what to do.

When he enters the cage Nero immediately retreats to the far corner, where he sits and eyes him nervously. Nero's shoulder is nearly as tall as his own, and his head is so enormous that Nathan is amazed he can carry it about, but Nero's fear is evident. Queen is slightly smaller but no less striking, for she carries herself with uncommon grace. She watches him with interest, and when he looks into her eyes, their beauty takes his breath away. They are an extraordinary colour: enormous liquid pools of molten gold, flecked with black. The absence of a mane makes them stand out even more, he thinks. How can one be sure of anything in this lion's eyes? Truly she is deserving of her name. He longs to be her ally, and has done so since he first laid eyes on her. He would love to run his hands along the marvellous curve of her frame.

Queen yawns, stretching her two front legs forward as far as they will go. She licks a paw with her enormous pink tongue and begins to clean the side of her jaw with it, almost mocking him with her relaxed stance. When she has finished she settles her gaze on him, and he could swear there is a glimmer of amusement in her eye. He takes a deep breath and steps towards her, raising the whip and cracking it loudly in the air. Queen rises to her feet, instantly obeying his signal, and gives a short snarl of assent. She trots over to the painted wooden pedestal and leaps upon it, settling herself surprisingly delicately. After a moment's hesitation, Nero follows her lead and climbs upon his. The lions watch Nathan patiently, awaiting their next cue.

Nathan exhales, for he is suddenly, enormously relieved. He takes another breath and musters all his concentration, shutting out the outside world. He begins to put the cats through their paces, using a series of verbal commands he learned from the tamer, a curious mix of words culled from English, French and Russian: the language of lions, laughed the tamer when he asked. Queen and Nero obey him perfectly, indeed they almost seem to enjoy themselves, and before he realises it, fifteen minutes have passed and the session is almost over. He pauses to catch his breath, feeling the sweat slowly trickle down his sides. The lions eye him expectantly, awaiting his next command, but he sees that he must leave the cage immediately, for the strength has suddenly left him.

He hears a noise behind him, the sound of something scraping against the ground on the far side of the menagerie, but he does not want to take his eyes from the lions. Queen and Nero's eyes move in unison to some point beyond his range of vision. The tent was empty when he started, and he swears silently to himself, for he does not wish the lions' concentration to stray. He takes a step backwards towards the cage door, and as he does so he hears the taut, clear voice of a woman several paces behind him.

'Anyone can enter a cage,' she says calmly. 'It is the leaving which is difficult.'

Nathan hesitates; she is right. The lions' attitude has shifted from obedience to measured interest. Nero jerks his head to one side and roars, a noise of bottomless depths accompanied by a deep grating tone that freezes Nathan's blood. He takes another cautious step backwards towards the door.

'By his very nature, a retreating man is a thing to be hunted,' says the voice behind him calmly. 'Even now they are stalking you. Can you see?'

Nathan nods mutely, for he can see only too clearly. Queen has lowered her head, and the fur along her back has risen upright.

'Breathe in deeply,' says the voice. 'Lift your chin and hold her gaze. Show her you are in control.' Nathan obeys the voice, just as Queen and Nero obeyed him only moments before. He takes a deep breath and swells his chest, raising the whip in a commanding manner.

'Now take three steps slowly backwards and you are at the door.' Nathan does this, senses the iron bars immediately behind him, and reaches his free hand back to undo the latch. His face feels hot, as if he is about to faint, and the lions swim before his eyes. He feels the latch slip free, and eases himself sideways out of the door, drawing it closed instantly. His hand trembles as he locks it, and when it finally clicks shut he rests his head upon the bars.

'Look at them now,' she says, her voice not five feet behind him. Nathan raises his eyes to Queen and Nero. 'They are indifferent, now that you're beyond their reach. Even bored.' She is right: Queen is cleaning herself, and Nero's head rests calmly on his forepaws.

'You must never turn your back on them,' she says.

Nathan slowly turns himself to face the speaker, and as he does so he has the sense that his entire life has been hurtling towards this moment. He sees her all at once: the heavy wooden chair with wheels, the thick mane of dark hair, now streaked with grey and piled high on her head, the starkly painted crimson of her lips, and the shrivelled legs with their thin straps of leather. His eyes finally come to rest on her feet, which are clothed only in dark woollen socks. They hang limply just above the ground. In his mind he sees the handbill, the image he has lived with all these years, and knows that his mother is here in front of him.

He meets her unsuspecting gaze.

'You're worked the cats before?' she asks.

'No.' His voice cracks slightly as he speaks, and he fears that it will betray him. Her hands rest lightly on the wheels of the chair, and she rotates them slowly forward, inching towards him. Her face is heavily lined and much fuller than he remembers. But she is still handsome, he thinks, even though she has lost the allure of her youth.

'You look as if you've done it all your life.' She says this matter-of-factly, and Nathan feels himself swell with pride. His face grows hot and he looks away, embarrassed. She ignores him, wheels herself deftly round his side to face Queen and Nero in the cage.

'Look at them,' she says. 'They are the most elegant, powerful creatures on earth. And the least worthy of your trust. They are like children.'

Nathan turns and sees the outline of her profile, feels the anger rise from deep within him. She turns back to him and smiles. Her teeth are small and well-formed, though stained now with age.

'But they must trust you absolutely, like a child does a parent. And in turn you must respect them. And fear them, just a little. The man who enters a cage without fear does not deserve to be there, for he does not appreciate their worth. A man who enters a cage without fear will soon be carried out of it. Do you understand?'

Nathan nods. He cannot bring himself to speak: what would he say?

'My husband was a tamer: the greatest tamer of his time. Mad Jack the Lion King, they called him. Perhaps you've heard of him,' she says expectantly.

Nathan shakes his head. She had a husband, he thinks.

She waves a hand. 'You are too young. He was the first to enter the cage without a gun. And the first to work them in groups of more than three. He loved his cats. They were like children to him. Even more than children.' She fixes her eye on him. 'Sometimes I think he loved them more than me.' She gives a thin trickle of a laugh, and Nathan hears in it the sound of his childhood.

He feels suddenly light-headed, as if he is in a dream.

'What's your name?' she asks.

He hesitates, for it was she who christened him Nathaniel. 'Nathan,' he says finally. He watches her closely, waiting for some sign of recognition, but she gives none.

'You should work them in the ring,' she says. 'With some training you'd be better than that drunkard. You're not a drinker, are you?'

'No, ma'am.'

'Good. It's always the booze that wrecks a tamer.'

'Is that what killed him?'

'Who?' She narrows her eyes at him, just as Queen does, and Nathan hesitates.

'Your husband.'

She stares at him for a long moment. 'No,' she says at last. 'It was fear that killed him. He lost his nerve.'

'I'm sorry.'

She blinks rapidly, then turns away. 'It was a long time ago. Things were different then . . .' Her voice tails off.

Yes, he thinks. For all of us.

'How much do they pay you?' she asks.

'Twenty shillings a week,' he says.

'I'll treble that. I'll train you myself. You can start tonight.'

He looks at her perplexed. 'Ma'am?'

'With them,' she says, nodding her head towards the cage. 'In the ring.'

He takes a deep breath, feeling a wave of nausea. It isn't just the lions he fears, it's the crowd. And her.

'I've never worked the ring,' he says tentatively.

She looks right at him, and when she speaks, she uses the tone of tamers. 'You will.'

12

Nathan

ATHAN HAS ONLY a few memories of her outside
the ring, but there is one he returns to again and
again. He has kept it with him so long that it is
tarnished with age, but still he cherishes it like a child covets
a cheap keepsake from the fair. In his mind, they lie next to
each other on a pile of old blankets in the back of a covered
wagon. The canvas shelters them but the wagon is open at the
rear, and a steady sheet of warm summer rain falls outside,
obscuring his view of the horizon. The road is thick with mud
and the wagon lurches from side to side as it rolls forward,
its pace no greater than that of a Sunday stroll. Now and then
the horses come to an abrupt halt, their harnesses jangling,
the wagon's heavy wooden wheels mired in the mud.
Lorenzo, the driver, shouts at them and curses, the water
cascading off the tilt of his beaten leather hat. He jumps
down from his perch and grabs hold of a bridle, dragging the
team forward, the horses' hoofs making great sucking sounds
in the mud, the wheels, as they roll through the puddles,

splattering his trouser legs. Nathan peeps through a rent in the canvas at him. Lorenzo's expression as he coaxes the horses is unyielding, determined – the way it is when he performs. Nathan knows that this is all part of the show: this movement from place to place is as much a part of it as the moment when the lights go up and the crowd stirs with anticipation. Nathan knows, even though he is only a child, that these people were born to move.

He buries his face in the blankets, feeling his sleeping mother's warmth next to him. The scent of moisture envelops him: the smell of damp canvas, musty blankets, wet horsehair, sodden prairie earth, and the musky odour of his mother's perspiration all mingle together in his nostrils. Far off in the distance he hears the faint crackle of thunder, but the sound is too remote to frighten him, nothing but the tiny pop of a child's cork gun across the vast prairie landscape. His mother stirs in her sleep and rolls over, one arm thrown above her head, and he stares at the soft white flesh along the inside of her forearm. He has an urge to lick it, to taste the clean skin of her, for his mother is like some rare delicacy that he is only occasionally allowed to savour. She does this to him: withholds herself. And perhaps because of this he loves her more than he should.

He has watched Maria, Lorenzo's wife, with their three children; has seen her idle caresses and fond looks, even while she scolds them. They climb aboard her like she herself is the wagon, clamber over her, settle themselves in the folds of her body without a thought. He watches them with envy, longing to touch his mother in the same familiar way, even though he knows he mustn't. She rarely holds him, only sometimes takes his hand, and when she does he holds on too tightly, fearful that she will let go. Once she scolded him for this, dropping his hand abruptly. 'You squeeze too hard,' she said. In that instant he hated himself.

She is beautiful. He knows this, for he has seen the men of the circus eyeing her as she puts her horses through their paces each morning, has seen them follow her with their gaze when she returns from the pump with a cotton rag twisted round her hair. Even their wives watch her, for he can sense that she is unlike them, made of something different altogether, though he does not know what. They treat her differently as well, are more polite but also more guarded in their manner. He's noticed that when she speaks to them it is always with a purpose. The other women laugh and chatter among themselves, but never to her. He wonders sometimes whether she misses this, the way he himself misses her caresses.

He sees a fork of lightning on the horizon, bright green flashing in the distance. A moment later, the crack of thunder follows, and this time it is loud enough to make him start. Without thinking he grabs his mother's arm, and she flinches in her sleep. The thunder growls again in the distance, and his mother's eyes flutter open. She looks at him and he releases her arm. She rolls over on to her stomach with a sigh, and reaches a hand up to his hair, gently stroking him. He holds his breath as she does, unable to believe his good fortune, closes his eyes and feels the warmth of her palm against his brow. Then the warmth disappears, and when he opens his eyes her hand has returned to her side.

'I love the rain in summer,' she murmurs. He looks at her

and she is smiling, even though her eyes are closed. Is she asleep? For a moment he cannot tell. She breathes in deeply, then exhales and opens her eyes and looks at him. He smiles a little in return, before realising that her gaze is not with him at all, but somewhere else, far away. 'It reminds me of home,' she says. A shadow darkens his face, for with this one word she closes another door to him. Only once or twice does he remember her using this word, and each time it unsettles him, for he does not know what she means. Their home is the wagon, or sometimes the canvas tent, or sometimes a house of lodging, or sometimes a cheap hotel. But this is not what she refers to and he knows it.

His mother sits up, rubs the sleep from her face with her long, slender hands, and twists the dark mass of hair, which has loosened in sleep, into a tight bun at the base of her neck. He watches her covertly as she does this, and she catches him out of the corner of her eye. She looks at him, and this time he knows for certain that it is him she sees. She appears to be weighing him up in her mind, the way one might judge a pastry before buying it. Her gaze is unsparing as she takes in all his details, his fine, dark eyebrows and matted tangle of hair. Gypsy hair, she called it, the colour of burned rope. His face was long for a child, with a sharply pointed chin and a solemn expression.

Finally she looks away and sighs again, a sound that makes him wince inwardly, for in it he can hear her longing. She stares out at the rain, chewing on her thumb, the coil of her hair already working its way loose, snaking down her long back.

'Perhaps one day I'll take you there,' she says absently.

13

Lulu

LULU AND NAN disappear inside the commode like naughty schoolgirls. It is a little ritual they share on Saturday nights when Lulu has finished his performance. Lulu procures a large glass of brandy for each of them from the bar, and they squeeze inside the tiny dressing room. Lulu strips off the bustier and uses a damp cloth to wipe the sweat from his face, taking care not to dislodge his hairpiece. Tonight he will take a chance and remain in women's garb, though he will change out of his performer's costume into something more appropriate for the after-hours club he frequents. He will have to avoid Talliot when he leaves, but what is life without its little risks?

Lulu has brought a dark red satin crinoline for the evening. He has had it made by an obliging seamstress (he pays doubly for her discretion) and when he pulls it from his bag Nan's eyes go round with admiration. He smiles and holds it up against her face and together they turn to the mirror, regarding her reflection. Nan has never worn an article of clothing so fine, and he can see that she is at once both disconcerted and entranced. After a moment's hesitation, she laughs and hands it back to him with a shake of her head.

Outside the crowd roars with laughter at the antics of the clowns, the last act before the show's finale. On Saturday nights the house is full to bursting and even the grim-faced Talliot walks with a spring in his step, in happy anticipation of the takings. Tonight Lulu and Nan must be doubly careful, for not only is Talliot about, but the old woman as well. Earlier that evening, Lulu stood in the doorway of the menagerie tent and watched as the old woman calmly informed the lion tamer he was no longer needed. The tamer was speechless at first, his crimson face bloated with drink. And then he spat at her dangling feet and cursed the lot of them, before stumbling out the door.

The old woman appeared completely unconcerned by this display, but not the cage boy. Nathan was quietly attending to one of the other animals at the time, but when the tamer had gone he stood completely still, his expression rigid. The old woman wheeled herself round in front of him and Nathan appeared almost frightened. She instructed him to forego the usual performance and simply to feed the lions for the audience. The old woman had an uncanny ability to read the crowd: they went wild when the boy threw the horsemeat at the lions. The boy himself seemed surprised, turned and looked at the eager faces with bewilderment, even as Queen and Nero tore into the bloody mass of flesh and bones.

Nan pulls another article of clothing from Lulu's bag. It is a velvet shoulder wrap of deepest blue, trimmed in white fur. Nan clasps it round her neck and smiles into the mirror and

Lulu catches a breath at her beauty. Nan laughs but Lulu orders her to hold still while he applies a little paint to her face: a bit of scarlet to her lips, a hint of blue shadow over the eyes, and perhaps just a trace of colour to her cheeks. When he is finished even Nan is impressed, for her expression grows suddenly serious in the mirror. After a moment she slowly removes the wrap from her shoulders and folds it carefully, tucking it safely back in the bag. Lulu shrugs and hands her the brandy and together they clink glasses. As Nan raises her glass to her lips, Lulu leans forward with a wry grin and murmurs a toast.

'To the boy tamer,' he says.

Nan smiles.

14

Nathan

NATHAN VOMITS IN the darkness outside the menagerie tent. It is fear that makes him ill or perhaps relief. He rests his forehead for a moment against the moist, cool canvas of the tent. He has done what he has long considered impossible: he has gone into the ring. He has stepped inside the neat circle of freshly strewn sawdust and seen the sea of faces all around him, heard their muffled gasps and cries of astonishment as he fed the lions, felt in the depth of his gut the reverberations of their rapturous applause.

All his life he has carefully skirted the ring's enclosure. He has seen himself as one who moved discreetly behind the scenes, quietly enabling others to perform. This image has suited him and he has cultivated it. But standing here in the darkness it strikes him that he was not responsible for it; it was imposed on him.

The first time he asked the Italians why he could not join them in the ring, they shook their heads and clicked their tongues and rolled their eyes with characteristic theatricality. It was Riza, the strongman, who finally confided in him when he was nearly seven. 'Your mother,' he told him one day with a shrug of his massive shoulders. 'She did not want you in the ring. It was her last request.' They always spoke of her this way, as if referring to the dead. Then Riza raised his eyebrows, as if to say: and who are we to oppose her, even though she had saddled us with the care of this young half-breed, who was neither from this country nor our own? Even in her absence they treated her with deference.

So to step inside the ring tonight was to deny his own past. His mother, however, could not have known this. Nathan is still reeling from that first encounter with her. In the moment when he spoke his name, some possibility was instantly curtailed. His name was the secret code meant to unlock their past. He had found her after all these years, and still she managed to evade him, just as she had always done.

He straightens and takes a deep breath, wipes a few stray specks of spittle from his lips with the back of his sleeve. He hears footsteps in the darkness behind him, and turns to see the orange girl standing there. He cannot remember her name. She is half hidden in shadow but he can still make out the look of concern upon her face.

'I'm sorry,' she says abruptly. 'I heard a noise.' She looks away, embarrassed.

He hears her strange lilting accent, different from those he's grown accustomed to these past two months. It is softer, more melodious, easier for him to understand.

'Are you all right?' she asks, when he does not reply. Her concern is genuine and touches him, for he has made no friends in this new country. He sees that she is pretty in a stark sort of way, and wonders for a fleeting moment why he never noticed her before.

She continues to stare at him. 'It's nothing,' he says finally, his words half choked in shame. She smiles a little, understanding his embarrassment.

'You did well tonight,' she says reassuringly. 'In the ring.'

He peers at her, wonders whether she is teasing him. He shakes his head, runs a hand self-consciously through his cropped hair. 'I survived,' he says.

'You did more than that,' she says. 'The crowd . . . they liked you. I could tell. They buy more oranges when they're excited.' She smiles again. 'It's the same with Lulu.'

He blushes at the mention of Lulu, as if this strange, dark-haired girl in front of him can see right through his skin to the naked core of his desire. Without thinking, he shuffles backwards a step, feels his heels strike an iron ring stuck fast into the earth.

'Anyway, you're a tamer now,' she says wryly.

A tamer, he thinks. He cannot master his own emotions, let alone the course of his own future. He longs to tell her that he came to this place in search of his mother but now that he has found her she is further from him than ever before; but he says nothing.

The girl eyes him for a moment. He notices then that she is wearing lip paint and eye make-up, thinks that he has never seen her with either before. Her long black hair is freshly combed and pulled back from her face. She has tucked a tiny flower, a rose bud, behind one ear. She bites her lip.

'You and Lulu are the lucky ones,' she says finally. Her eyes are large and serious. 'As long as you perform well, you'll keep your place. It's different with the rest of us. We're nothing to her. She could be shot of us tomorrow if she wanted.'

Nathan does not know how to read this girl, and does not know why she has chosen to confide in him in a land where people keep their confidences. He wants to reassure her, just as she has reassured him, but knows that he cannot.

'You are wrong,' he says softly, shaking his head with certainty. 'She needs none of us.' And then he turns and walks away, leaving the orange girl and her smell of citrus behind him in the darkness.

15

Nan

ON SATURDAY NIGHTS, Nan goes to the New Cut. It is not half a mile from Lambeth Walk, and there she can drink and dance and forget herself for a time. She chooses one of the better drinking-houses that have sprung up near the Victoria Theatre, and treats herself to a plate of oysters, and a glass of Moselle. She always pays for it out of her earnings, unlike the score of slatternly girls ranged along the brightly lit bar. Nan prizes her independence above all else, for she knows how easily it can be lost.

Tonight the Moselle disappears too quickly. She orders a second and moves to a spot near the door, where she can watch the night's activities. The street outside is packed with throngs of costers: men, women, children of all ages, hawking everything from sprats to shoelaces. Night makes them bold. They shout and shove with equal vigour, for what they do not sell they'll have to carry home and make a bed with. These are her mother's people, though she feels not an ounce of loyalty to them. Her mother was one of them, but they did nothing to help her in the end, when she looked inside a bottle and disappeared.

That is the way of costers, thinks Nan. Already those outside are flush with drink. And the young boys, those who've not yet taken to the bottle themselves, look for opportunity. Nan watches as a lad of six or seven weaves his way around the crowd, slipping in and out unseen. He is dark with dirt and wears a man's woven cap pulled down low, past his ears. But his eyes are keen and his face is not as pinched as some. In the next moment she sees him snatch a hot potato from beneath the seller's eye. He disappears so quickly that she wonders for an instant whether her mind did not conjure him. The boy will burn his fingers, she thinks, but his belly will be full, even if he must forego the salt and slab of butter.

That is the fate we leave our children: to snatch life out from under one another. And her boy would have done the same, no doubt, had he survived. So perhaps it's better that he didn't, she thinks ruefully. Now, however, she must reckon with his ghost. He haunts her even here, in the crowded alleys of the New Cut. Nan closes her eyes and takes a deep draught of Moselle. When she opens them, a chinless barmaid sets a plate of oysters down in front of her. They are small and round and dark as tarnished silver, salty to the taste. Oysters were her father's dish. She eats them in his memory.

Her father was a tosher, a shore man who salvaged what he could from London's sewers. Nan hated the idea of it, and as a child often dreamed of rats the size of wild boars. But her father preferred the work to any other, and thought nothing of the foul circumstances in which he laboured. 'It isn't such a bad place,' he often mused. 'There's naught below men's feet but what's above, only more of it.' Nan was exceedingly fond of him, though even as a child she could see he was peculiar. One day when she was fifteen he went below and never surfaced, held fast by the muck and filth of generations.

She swallows the oysters whole, the way he taught her, sucking the brine from each shell in turn. They are soft and cool, and when she tastes them she can almost forget that six days out of seven she eats herring. She eats them quickly, and when she tips the last one past her lips, she hears his voice. She almost chokes.

'Still oysters and Moselle.'

He has appeared suddenly behind her, the way he used to as a child. He wears the blue wool suit of a sailor, and his face is burnished from the sun. The colour suits him, though she wishes that it didn't. She has forgotten how tall he is, though she can see that he has grown even thinner in the past year. The sailor's suit hangs loosely from his frame. His pale hair is shorn close, and his face carries a fine layer of golden hair. He looks older, as if he's finally lost the glaze of boyhood. Her eyes drift down to his hand, splayed about the pint glass. Even his hands seem larger, she thinks, frowning. They are long and thin, well worn with weather.

'You see, Nan? Nothing ever changes.' He says this with the fervour of youth, as if he is the first to discover it.

'You're wrong, Shad. Everything changes.'

He looks her over. 'Not you.'

Lulu's make-up is still on her face. She does not want Shad to see her painted like a harlot. She pulls a soiled kerchief from her pocket and, as quickly as she can, wipes her lips and cheeks, bending down towards the bar. When she lifts her face again, it is pink with embarrassment. Shad looks at her knowingly.

'You're alone.'

'What of it?'

He smiles. 'Like the last time. On the steps.'

Nan thinks of the last time Shad fell into her life, on the steps of St Paul's. 'Don't start, Shad.'

'But we never finished,' he says earnestly. 'You just disappeared.' She looks at him, and this time she sees a boy of four, angry that she's hidden from him once again.

Nan lifts her glass and drinks. If only she could disappear. Shad lifts his pint and downs it in one long pull. Out of the corner of her eye, Nan watches the rhythmic bulging of his throat as he swallows. She has never settled with the sight of Shad and a drink.

'I thought you'd gone to sea,' she says finally.

'It threw me back,' he says with a sheepish smile.

She shakes her head. She is hardly surprised, for Shad has never been able to keep to anything. She nods at his sailor's uniform. 'What of your clothes?'

He shrugs. 'They're all I've got.'

She sighs. 'They'll draw and quarter you, Shad.'

'They won't bother. I wasn't much use anyway.' He makes a swaying motion with his body, as if he can't find his sea legs, and she laughs. 'I guess I'm land-locked now,' he says then. 'I guess we both are.'

She stops laughing. His eyes are fixed on her in a way that makes her uneasy. She hears the music float up from down below. Impulsively he takes her by the elbow and pulls her to her feet.

'Give us a dance, Nan. Just the one.'

She starts to protest, but already he is leading her through the crowd towards the stairway that leads to the darkened dance hall below. He offers the sixpence to enter, and together they descend the steep stone stairs to the crowded floor. The room is large and cavernous, with sloping ceilings like a cave. The walls have been painted a deep burgundy and the ceiling has been festooned with a garland of coloured lights. A small group of musicians huddles at one end of the room and a long bar lines the other. There are more people here than she can count: costers mainly, women in worn print dresses, and thick-soled boots that land heavily upon the wooden floor, their necks draped in their partners' scarves. A group of sailors dominates the bar, for the Thames is but a few hundred yards away. They dance lewdly with gaudily dressed women. Every so often the women pause and call for gin in too-loud voices, their cheeks crusty with powder and rouge. They drink it neat in half-pint glasses, their eyes shimmering with intoxication.

Nan watches them, until Shad grabs her and gives her a little spin. She laughs again, in spite of herself, for he has always had the ability to startle her. And then he pulls her in close, and she feels his face in her hair, and his warm breath upon her neck. He inhales deeply, as if he is trying to steal some vital part of her, and at once she stiffens. Her smile fades. He's come upon her quickly, like a rush tide. If she isn't careful, she'll get caught. To her relief, the song ends quickly, and when the music stops, she takes a step backwards, easing him away. She has the sudden sensation of being trapped like an animal, cannot help but look around the room for a means of escape. And that is when she sees the cage boy standing in the corner, his eyes trained on her intently. She meets his gaze and, for an instant, she is reminded of the way he looks at Queen. She wonders whether he has followed her.

A man lurches in between, obscuring her view, and when she turns back towards Shad he sees that something is amiss.

'What is it?'

He does not like to think that others have the power to unsettle her. Quickly he scans the room, but does not see the source of her discomfort. He turns back to her, his face now dark with irritation.

'C'mon. Let's go.' Once again he's got her by the hand and is pulling her through the crowd. Nan hesitates, reluctant now to leave, but dares not turn her eyes towards the cage boy. Shad senses her unwillingness, and pulls a little harder.

And then they are on the stairs, and she can feel the drag of her body against his. She climbs as slowly as she can, and when she is near the top she allows herself one last glance over her shoulder. Nathan's eyes remain fixed on her.

16

Nathan

NATHAN HAS NOT followed her. He's been to the New Cut many times before, likes to lose himself in the noise and jostle of the crowds. Tonight he came here to forget his mother. And now he wishes that he hadn't. As he looks across the room towards Nan's retreating figure, he cannot help but feel that fate has played a cruel joke on him. For he is suddenly, almost painfully, aware of his solitude.

He realises now that he had not expected his mother to change. Her restless beauty, her cold spirit, even her some-times brutal indifference – he wanted only those things he'd once possessed as a child. But age and circumstances have rendered her a stranger. Now his mother does not know him, and Nathan does not know what to do with his memory of her.

The one thing he recognises is her voice: its almost gravelly tone, low for a woman, and its imperiousness. Her voice is with him, locked inside his head, even though he has come to the New Cut to escape it. But he hadn't counted on meeting anyone he knew, for he is still strangely out of place in this city. He saw Nan almost straight away from his position in the corner, watched her descend the stairs on the arm of a sailor nearly two heads taller than himself. He saw the young man pull her towards him in a tight clench of familiarity. These two are well acquainted, he thought with wry envy. He saw the sailor bend his head right down to nestle into hers: read something in that incline, a childish gesture of longing. He saw her spine stiffen in response. Perhaps she was not given to such public displays, or perhaps her reaction indicated something different altogether.

Then she spotted him. He blushed foolishly in the darkness, knowing that he should simply nod and look away. But he could not take his eyes from them, even when she herself was forced to turn away. On the stairs the girl craned her neck back at him, her eyes darting anxiously towards the corner where he stood. He recognised the look in them, and felt a familiar flutter of desire.

During his last year with the mud circus, the troupe had reassembled after a bitter cold winter of rambling. Those that were unattached had lined up one morning to pair off for the season in an annual ritual known as Choosing Day. Gina, a newly widowed acrobat, had been among the first to choose. She had boldly linked her arm in his, defying the maternal stares of Carla and Maria and the others, not to mention his own bewildered gaze, and had calmly led him back to her wagon. Nathan had been struck dumb at the time, had seen his life veer abruptly in an unexpected direction.

He had never lain with a woman before, had never even

kissed one. He knew he'd been a little slow in this respect. Gina had been drawn to his innocence. She knew that in his virgin arms she'd find a balm for the aching wound that had opened in her life. She was more than twice his age: he with no more than a rumour of hair upon his chin, and she with a tiny patchwork of lines about each eye that disappeared only partly when she slept. Once alone in her wagon Gina had taken his hand and guided it gently towards her breast. And he'd found to his surprise that what she lacked in youth or beauty she made up for in the sheer depth of her allure.

He remembers the tremor in his fingers as he'd undressed that first night by the flickering light of a tallow candle: the heady mix of fear and shame and adolescent desire, a feeling so strong he thought it must show on his face. Gina had known, and pulled him to her breast, stroking his hair the way a mother does. Little by little, he had discovered himself within the confines of her flesh: his own desire. Once she'd uncorked him, he'd thought that he'd explode. She had laughed when he came that first night, not a cruel laugh, but a celebratory one, and he too had laughed; from relief. I am normal, he had thought. A man like any other.

He'd settled quickly into the rhythm of their life together, enduring her frequent bouts of grief with equanimity. Despite her passion, he knew that it was not him she wanted, but her dead husband. The intimacy he shared with her did not rival what she'd had. He remained in awe of her past. It was about this time that the dreams returned: he began to dream nightly of his mother in the ring. Gina would rouse him gently in the middle of the night, cool the sweat upon his brow with the flat of her palms. He'd wake suddenly, the warm scent of the prairie reminding him who he was, and gaze up into Gina's face. My mother, he would think.

He did not tell Gina of his dreams, but he wondered afterwards whether she hadn't known from the start. Indeed, he wondered whether they hadn't all understood: Gina, Riza, Carla and the others. They had not been surprised when he told them he was leaving. They had nodded and wished him well, as if he was merely acting out the next chapter in a story written long before.

17

Nan

OUTSIDE THE DANCE hall, Nan feels herself sliding towards a place she should not be. She pushes Shad away. 'I must go,' she says urgently.

'Why?' Shad replies evenly. He steps forward and slides his hands round her waist. 'Stay on awhile.'

'I can't,' she says.

'Where do you have to be, Nan?'

She looks around her. There is nowhere and he knows it. He has always known it. The lack of anything else in her life has left her exposed to him, even after all this time.

'You can't leave now,' he murmurs into her ear. 'I came back to find you. Nothing's changed, you see? We're both still here.'

She looks at him. Everything has changed, she thinks desperately, but she fears that he is right.

'Please, Nan, don't leave me again.'

Nan shakes her head and tries to back away, but does not try hard enough. Something in her cannot refuse him, for he is still the father of her son. He pulls her to him once again, bends his head down to find her lips. She feels the softness of his young man's whiskers against her skin, tastes the warmth of him, feels her body tense. She has not touched a living soul these past twelve months, not since she relinquished the tiny body of the boy.

'Please, Nan,' he murmurs into her ear. 'Just tonight.'

She kisses him deeply, her head cloudy with Moselle, and her mind flies to the cage boy.

18
Lulu

L ULU PAUSES JUST outside the doorway of the menagerie tent. It is mid-afternoon, and for once the godforsaken English sun has managed to penetrate the sulphurous brown haze. He draws aside the canvas flap that covers the door and peers inside the darkness, straining to catch a glimpse of the cage boy at his chores. Lulu takes more risks these days, lingers around the tent at odd times in hope of a chance meeting. Nathan often works the lions at this hour, when the site is deserted. Sometimes he practises alone, sometimes with the old woman directing him from her chair.

It is more than three weeks since she fired the tamer, and the boy has been hard at work ever since, putting the lions through their paces two or three times each day. Lulu can tell from the glint in her eye that the old woman is pleased: she treats the boy with affected indifference, but it is apparent to everyone except Nathan that she has taken an interest in him. Perhaps he reminds her of her dead husband. Or perhaps she is drawn to his youth and beauty. If so, she must wait her turn, he thinks.

The boy was born to work with animals, to be sure. He handles the lions with ease now. Lulu envies Queen and Nero this intimacy. He hated the lion act in the past: he'd regarded those who tame animals as beneath him, believing that there was no grace or skill to such acts, only showmanship. These men longed to be heroes, subduing both the audience and their captives with lashes and harsh words. In reality, they were fools.

He owes this view in part to his father. Lulu's father was a consummate performer, a magician and acrobat who could command the attention of an entire crowd simply by raising an eyebrow. It was Lulu's father who taught him that animal acts were unchristian and immoral: a performing animal is broken, he used to say. Its spirit must be shattered before it enters the ring.

Nathan, however, is not like the others. When he enters the ring it is not as an adversary; he moves and thinks the way the lions do, performs with them. He exhibits none of the awkwardness that plagues him in his dealings with people, nor any of the treachery or drunken cowardice of his predecessor. Even his figure alters: he seems to grow six inches in the ring, and age several years. He becomes less pretty, Lulu thinks, but more desirable.

Lulu watches his act each night from the wings, just as Nathan himself watches Lulu. He knows Nathan buries himself each night deep within the crowd while he flies overhead. Nan has told him this; has tossed this morsel of knowledge to him casually, the way she might a piece of fruit.

And though he confides a great deal in Nan, he has not let her glimpse the depth of his affection for the boy. He guards this feeling carefully; his devotion is far too rare and fragile a commodity to be bantered about lightly between friends. He can hardly bear to contemplate what might happen if his feelings were reciprocated by the boy, though the idea gives him pleasure in his dreams. For the moment at least, Lulu is content to admire Nathan from afar.

Now Lulu squints into the darkness of the tent, his eyes struggling to find their focus. He can see the orang-utan asleep in a bed of straw not far from where he stands, but can make out little else. He is just about to turn away when something catches his eye, a movement within the lion cage, a flash of human hair. He steps inside the flap noiselessly and presses his body against the canvas walls. He edges sound-lessly along the perimeter of the tent for some distance until the lion cage comes into view. He sees Nero sleeping in the corner on the flat of his side, his enormous paws stretched out in front of him. And he sees the long line of Queen's shoulder as she reclines with her back to him, her tail casually brushing the air like sea kelp waving on the tide.

Then a hand appears, delicately tracing the curve of her spine. Lulu holds his breath, and in the silence that follows he can just make out the sound of Queen's contented purring. It is the thrum of a thousand tiny strings reverberating in the darkness. The sound seems to swell and envelop him; it reaches right inside him until Lulu feels the vibration deep within his own body. He closes his eyes, and becomes the lioness. He can feel the boy's lingering hand along his torso, can feel his own desire stiffen in response. Surely this boy will slay him with his languid looks and long caress. After a time Queen ceases purring, and Lulu opens his eyes. He sees the lioness give her head a little shake as Nathan's hand scratches her round the ears, then watches as the boy slowly raises himself up to a sitting position. Nathan's eyes dart across the darkness to Lulu's hiding place against the wall, and Lulu thinks he sees a flicker of recognition. Nathan holds his pose expertly, making no sudden movement or sound, and Lulu realises that by his very presence he puts the boy in danger. He stands paralysed, locked in Nathan's gaze, and then the boy gives the barest ghost of a nod towards the doorway. Lulu begins to ease himself slowly sideways towards the canvas flap at the entrance to the tent. Not once does Nathan take his eyes away, and Lulu does not falter in his movement. He can do nothing but obey.

19

Nathan

A MOMENT LATER Nathan emerges, blinking, from
the tent. His heart is beating hard, though he
cannot tell if it is with anger or anticipation. More
and more he does not know himself outside the cage. He
cannot fathom his own emotions, nor can he make sense of
his own place within the society of others. These days it is
only the lions he understands: Queen and Nero, and their
savage, awesome, intoxicating, presence, and his own insatia-
ble need to be with them. He has even come to crave their
smell: the hotly acrid reek that greets him whenever he
enters the tent.

He scans the narrow street outside for Lulu, but finds it
deserted. He feels suddenly relieved. He is brave enough to
lie with lions but does not trust himself with the rope dancer.
He has seen Lulu lurking outside the tent, and the way he
watches him in the ring. Nathan is not fool enough to mistake
the lovesick look in Lulu's eyes. He wonders what the others
think, whether they too have noticed: Talliot, Karl, his

mother, Nan. Perhaps especially Nan. Since that night in the
New Cut, Nan will not meet his gaze, even though he has
made a point of nodding to her once or twice after the show.
He even bought an orange from her, but his hands shook so
much when he handed her the penny that he has not repeated
his mistake.

He retreats inside the tent. The darkness and scent of
animals surround him, and soothe his troubled mind. He
enters Kezia's cage, and begins to clear out her straw. The
orang-utan regards him carefully from a distance. She will
not allow him near her – refuses any human contact – and
Nathan does not force her friendship. Whatever happened to
her in the past he knows he cannot undo.

It is different with Queen. From the very first Nathan felt
a bond with the lioness that he cannot explain. He had never
touched either lion before, but knew that it was possible. He'd
been told that the very best tamers, the lion kings,
could stroke their cats, could sit astride them, could even lie
down with them. Nathan did not know whether he would
ever trust Nero in this way, but he longed to prove himself
with Queen.

While she is quick to obey his signals in the ring, Nathan
feels that it is Queen who controls him through the sheer
force of her presence. She willed him to enter the cage this
afternoon, and lifted her head immediately, almost as if she'd
been expecting him, while Nero slept the sleep of the dead.
She permitted him to lie next to her and run his hand along
her frame. He marvelled at the touch of her: the indescrib-
ably silky texture of her luxurious golden coat, and the
complex rope of muscles that lay beneath. He even raised her

paws and ran his thumbs over their velvet pads, sensing the razor-sharp claws retracted within. Most of all he felt his entire body resound with the deep reverberation of her content. Her response took his breath away: he had rarely felt such complete acceptance.

He hears a sound in the darkness behind him and turns to see Talliot wheel his mother through the door. He feels his mouth go dry. It has been three weeks since they first met, but her presence still unsettles him. Talliot often delivers her in this way, for she cannot negotiate the street outside alone. Nathan has learned that she owns the row of houses behind the circus, though he does not know which one she occupies, only that Talliot is never far from her side. He wonders at their relationship, for Talliot seems to jump whenever she commands, though he does not appear to be a cowering man.

Once inside the tent, she waves Talliot away. Nathan finishes cleaning Kezia's cage while his mother wheels herself round to face the lions. She has no interest in the other animals; indeed he has noticed that she has little interest in the circus itself, apart from occasional lectures to the equestriennes when she feels their performance has been poor. She rolls herself right up to the bars and peers inside.

'Queen's performance has been sluggish lately,' she says. 'Have you noticed?'

Nathan glances up and frowns. He has noticed a slight change in Queen's behaviour when she performs, though he has been loath to admit it. His mother watches him, awaiting his response. He shrugs. 'Perhaps it's the meat,' he offers lamely. 'Perhaps she needs more bone.'

His mother throws back her head and laughs. Nathan

colours. Inside the cage, Nero wakens at the sound. He sits up, shakes his enormous head, and gives a brief, irritated, snarl. Nathan's mother rolls her chair backwards a few feet, then rotates round to face him. 'Men are always the last to realise,' she remarks casually, a little note of triumph in her voice. 'Queen is expecting,' she says then. 'Did you not know?'

Nathan looks from her to Queen and back again. He feels something snap inside him. 'No,' he says, unable to lie. 'No, I did not.' In that instant, he feels that he has lost Queen to his mother.

She offers him a little smile of condescension. She has withheld this information from him until now, though he does not know why. Perhaps it is a kind of test. Nathan picks up the rush broom once again and begins to sweep the floor outside the cage.

'It is her first litter,' she continues. 'The cubs will be born soon. Before the New Year, if all goes according to plan.' Nathan glances at her. She speaks of Queen's pregnancy as if she's orchestrated the event, the way a tamer does a perform-ance. Queen rises up then, stretches her forepaws out in front of her as far as they will go, arching her back and dipping her pregnant belly towards the ground. She straight-ens then and wanders slowly over to the shallow pan of drinking water in the corner, the loose bulge of her under-side wobbling as she walks. She collapses heavily on to her haunches with a grunt and begins to lap the water. Nathan stares at her. Now that he's been told, her swollen abdomen seems obvious. How could he have overlooked it?

'If we're fortunate, the litter will be large,' continues his mother. 'Three or four, perhaps. The cubs will fetch a handsome price on the open market. The Americans will stop at nothing at the moment. They have no sense of scale. Everything must be big in America.' Nathan looks at her, hears the note of disdain in her voice. She forgets for the moment that he is American. 'Perhaps we'll add one of the litter to your act. If Queen is willing,' she adds reflectively. 'Not every lioness will tolerate the presence of her offspring in the ring.'

Nathan looks at her askance, but she appears oblivious. 'At any rate,' she continues, 'we shall have to take into account her breeding period. She will not be able to work for some weeks while she looks after the cubs. Nero will have to carry the show independently when she litters. Nero and you, of course.' She smiles at him then, and Nathan can see her perfect row of small teeth. 'Perhaps we shall teach you a new trick or two. Something different. Something that will make the audience gasp.' She smiles again enigmatically.

Nathan feels his pulse quicken. He looks at Nero, trying to see him in this new light. Nero is crouched not far from Queen. His enormous mane surrounds his head like a shaggy wreath. Nathan does not relish the idea of working Nero without Queen, but he cannot reveal this to his mother, as if it is a weakness he must hide. He hates this, the need to prove himself in her eyes. He has a sudden image of himself upon the painted pedestal in the ring, his mother brandishing the whip.

'There is so much more that we could do,' she continues. Her tone is excited and her eyes shimmer in the half-light of the tent. 'You've only learned a fraction of what is possible.

78

My husband used to say there is no limit but our conscience to what we can achieve within the ring.' Nathan frowns. She has not spoken of her husband since that first day, and there is much he'd like to ask her.

'And courage,' he adds unthinkingly. She turns to him and Nathan feels his face redden. The words have flown out of his mouth like starlings.

'That goes without saying,' she says. Her voice is flat now, cold. Nathan thinks of her dead husband.

'Conscience and courage are the same,' she says pointedly. 'Without them, we are lost.'

20
Nan

IT IS HER earliest memory. She is standing in the hallway, and can see her mother and Auntie stretched side by side upon the bed, the tiny bundle lodged between them. They call him Shad, like the roe. A sort of joke between them, though she doesn't know why. Come and meet your cousin, they call to her. She hesitates, for she doesn't like the sickly sweet smell from within. But she is curious, so she crosses slowly to the bedside, peering down at the wrinkled yellow face. She has seen babies who remind her of the smooth, pale petals of a flower, but this one looks like an old marrow. She tells them so, and her mother reaches out and gives her face a slap. The two women murmur something to each other and laugh. It is breakfast time and they are already flush with drink, celebrating the birth of a boy.

She watches him grow. Her mother and Auntie sing to him in lilting voices. As if there's never been a boy child on this earth, Nan thinks darkly. His eyes remain a bright blue, and after many months a thin layer of golden hair appears, but otherwise there is little to hold her interest. He sleeps away the days, and when he wakes, Auntie squeezes a few drops between his lips from a small brown bottle. She smiles as she does this, strokes the side of his cheek with the tips of her fingers. One day when Auntie takes him out, Nan finds the bottle and pulls out the stopper, sniffing at the contents. She takes a small sip, then spits the bitter taste upon the floor. She does not want to sleep.

Later, he learns to walk. He trails her doggedly, his forehead crinkled tight, and in the end she takes to felling him. He goes down easily, with nothing more than a shove of one hand, until one day she pushes and he falls against a step. His forehead splits like the skin of a tomato. When Nan looks inside the wound, she can see bone. Auntie locks her in the cupboard, telling her to take her time. She can hear Shad fretting in the next room, can hear him call her name again and again. Nan balls herself up like a fist, and falls asleep thinking of the things that she could do to him.

By the time he is four, he is left in her care, while her mother and Auntie slip away in search of drink. She watches from the doorway as they disappear, arm in arm, down the street. The two women are cousins, but they might as well be twins, for they have never lived apart. Nan envies them their pairing, wishes she had a sister instead of Shad. The boy still carries a mark from the day she pushed him over. It seems to grow with him, getting bigger every year. A token of affection, laughs her father. Nan hates the scar. One night when she and Shad are left alone, she tries to scrub it clean. She rubs and rubs until Shad shouts with pain. The skin on his face turns bright red, but the scar glows even whiter than before.

She makes him do her bidding. One day she orders him to steal an apple, and when he is caught she watches as the vendor smacks his open palm several times with a stick. Shad bites his lip and looks at her but doesn't cry. Afterwards, she pries open his fingers and stares down at the puffy red skin. She asks him if it hurts and he shakes his head slowly. He tells her he will try again, if that is what she wants. 'Don't be daft,' she says.

He grows like a weed. By the time she is eight, he is a head taller than she, though he is barely six. He remains thin and sallow. His eyes are large and pale blue and his tawny hair curls about his ears in long tendrils. But Shad is unlike other children, even Nan can see this. He seldom speaks to others and rarely smiles, and does not run with boys of his own age. When Nan is nine, they are both sent to school. Nan learns her letters quickly and is bored. Day after day, she fills her slate with made-up stories. By the time she writes the last word, she has already had to wipe away the first. Her stories have an end or a beginning, but never both.

Shad is not so lucky. After six months, his letters still look like writhing worms. The teacher singles him out, standing behind his chair, and hissing into his ear. After a year, he can barely write his name. The teacher sends a letter home saying he should not return. Auntie squints at the thin sheet of paper and passes it to Nan. When Nan reads it out loud, Auntie swears. In a gesture of loyalty, Nan is taken from the school as well.

Shad is sent to help his father with the fish, while she is kept at home to clean and cook and do what needs. At the end of the day, Shad wears the stink of the river. When she teases him, he only glowers. But later, she finds her slate in pieces on the floor. That year Auntie has another baby, a little girl they christen Fleur. The child wails incessantly, and the flat feels suddenly smaller. At the insistence of Nan's father, Auntie and her family move to rooms across the road. The day they leave, the two women clutch each other and weep.

When Fleur is one, Auntie takes her in the skiff across the Thames. Though they have managed well enough in the past, this time they fall foul of a steamer. The skiff snaps like a matchstick, and Auntie and the child both perish. Nan's mother is bereft. She spends her days in a darkened room, clutching a bottle to her breast, as if it were an infant. Now it is Nan who sells the oranges, for she cannot bear to be alone in the house with her mother. She seldom sees Shad, for the two families have been severed by death. But she no longer feels spite towards him, only pity.

The following spring, Shad's father decides to return to Plymouth, the city of his birth. Nan and her father help them load their things into a cart, and when they are finished, Shad climbs on top and folds his gangly limbs like a grasshopper. Nan watches as the cart lurches forward and then slowly rumbles round the corner. At the last moment, it is Nan who raises her hand to wave goodbye.

21

The Lions

QUEEN WATCHES THE cage boy undress by the flickering light of a candle. He is thin and muscular, like a young male gazelle. He bathes himself in a small hand basin that he has filled with water from the kettle, and as he cups the water to his face, she can see the soft, pale arc of flesh along his sides. Her eyes are drawn to this instinctively; she knows how easily the boy's flesh would give way, how little resistance it would offer to the razor of her claw. She knows it even as he enters the cage each night to stroke her, carries the fact of it inside her like a seed.

She is the object of much attention these days. The old woman comes to see her each morning and each evening, to gaze at her in silence, though Queen does not know why. The others pause by the cage and call to her, offer her their smiles and baffling words through the bars. Queen is puzzled by their sudden interest, and not a little wary. Even the cage boy has taken to sleeping in the menagerie tent of late. He makes up a bed by the coal stove each night after the others have gone home, and stokes the fire just before he sleeps, his face glowing red in the reflection of the flame. She admires him for this: he does not fear the flame as she does, but seems drawn to its lethal warmth. She thinks of the power in her claws, and the boy's ability to tame the fire, and cannot help but wonder which of them is stronger.

She tolerates the boy, but with Nero she is increasingly short-tempered. He has not mounted her in weeks, not since the night she caught his shoulder with a claw. He looked at her in shock that night, his eyes hazed with disbelief, even as the blood beaded up through his fur. Since then he has kept his distance, though Queen has noticed with irritation how he mopes about the cage.

She is secretly alarmed by the changes that are wreaking havoc in her body, and irritated by the hardness of the floor against her swollen belly. She has the feeling that if she could only return to the long grass of the veldt, then it would all make sense: the heaviness in her torso, the scrambling in her abdomen, and perhaps most of all, the distorted state of her mind, which makes everything around her shimmer as if filtered through a hazy wave of heat.

But she is not on the veldt; she is here with Nero in the cage. It is not warm here but cold, and the air does not contain the scent of other animals but the dense fumes of paraffin and burning coal, together with the stench of her own urine. The tightening in her belly conceals a burden that is pulling her ever downwards towards the earth. When she sits on her pedestal in the ring she feels dizzy, as if the floor below her has suddenly plummeted. She no longer has the energy to perform, nor the interest, and at night she sleeps only fitfully, waking often to gaze out into the darkness that surrounds the iron bars.

The other night she was woken by the boy's strangled cry. She was on her feet at once, staring out into the darkness of the tent, her eyes searching for him protectively. She saw him sitting hunched over on his makeshift bed, his chest heaving from some unknown terror. That night the boy came into the cage again, stood for what seemed an eternity watching Queen from the corner, and then finally eased himself down by her side. He laid his hands upon her abdomen with the utmost care, as if the thing inside her could somehow heal his wounds, and Queen remembers the warmth within his fingers, and the delicate feel of them upon the soft skin of her underbelly. That night she felt briefly reassured.

At other times she feels the panic rise within her. The old woman makes her feel this way. With her withered limbs and steely gaze, she seems grotesque. The boy, too, does not seem to trust her. Queen can almost feel the quickening in his chest when the old woman appears. He becomes mute in her presence. Yesterday the old woman came in the middle of the afternoon, when the tent was deserted. The boy was out, and even Nero was asleep in the corner of the cage, and Queen had the feeling that the world outside had closed in upon them, leaving her and the old woman to face each other in the half-light. To Queen's surprise, the old woman reached inside a bag and withdraw a large chunk of horseflesh, which she tossed into the cage not far from where Queen stood. The old woman spoke to her in muted tones, which Queen found instantly unsettling. She had the sudden sense of impending danger, the way she used to on the veldt when all at once the birds startled up into the sky.

Queen would not eat the meat, but let it lay upon the floor and retreated to the far side of the cage. The old woman grew angry, shouting at her through the bars and tapping on them sharply with a stick. Queen sat quietly through this display, glad for once of the iron cage that separated them. But the noise woke Nero, who rose with a start and in an instant devoured the lump of meat on the floor. The old woman watched wordlessly as he did this, her gaze hardening in Queen's direction.

22

Nan

A T HALF-PAST FIVE on Wednesday morning Nan jostles with the others at Houndsditch Market. Duke's Place is a large, square yard with iron gates and a string of dilapidated shopfronts. Already the street is littered with smashed fruit and jagged bits of walnut shells. A few scraggly hens roam the yard, scavenging among the piles of dried leaves that have been used to pack the oranges. It is a dreary place, devoid of colour, but the oranges here are cheaper than those at Covent Garden and the quality better. The Jews that run the place bargain as if their lives depended on it – it is said that in a good week their profits will run to hundreds. Nan does not know whether this is true, but she's made friends among the traders and knows how to strike a deal with flattery and a smile.

Nan likes it here. She feels an odd sort of longing for these people, and envies them their closeness. The women, she has noticed, are never alone. She can see into their houses, watches them crouch on richly coloured carpets in groups of three or four, jiggling tiny, dark-skinned infants on their laps. Every so often there is a burst of laughter that reaches right inside her. She wonders how they managed to plant themselves so deeply here.

The weather is bitter cold and the coffee sellers have set up early. The scent of freshly roasted coffee mingles with the sour smell of rotting citrus. She finishes haggling with the seller and shoulders her loaded basket. She picks her way through the crowd towards the cart she's left on the outskirts of the yard. Half a dozen paces from her cart she stops short, for she sees Shad there beside it, his eyes scanning the crowd. It is four days since she spent the night with him, but the fact of it is like an angry sore. She longs to take back the oysters and Moselle and the dancing.

She thinks of flight, but Shad spies her in the crowd. He moves quickly to her side and, without a word, lifts the basket proprietorially from her shoulder to his own. She leads him back to her cart and he lowers the basket to the ground.

'You didn't say goodbye,' he says.

Nan thinks of how she slipped away from his bedside in the chilling silence of the dawn. She looks him in the eye. 'That's because you never listen.'

Shad smiles. He raises both his hands and places them gently on each side of her head, cupping his palms against her ears, shutting out the noises of the market. It is a gesture from their childhood, and Nan listens for a moment to the whoosh of her own blood.

'Can you hear it?' he asks. She nods, then slowly reaches up and takes his hands and lowers them to his side.

'Go back to Plymouth.'

He shakes his head. 'I belong here. With you.'

Nan doesn't answer. Instead she bends down and begins to transfer the oranges by the handful into her cart. They are small and firm this time of year, their juice only slightly sour, and she will sell them two a penny. Shad watches for a moment, then squats down beside her and murmurs into her ear.

'You felt it, Nan. The other night. I know you did.'

She blushes, feeling a twist in her gut, for he is right. She did respond to his caress that night.

'Please, Shad. Let me be.'

'I can't,' he says.

'You must.'

'But I don't want to,' he says stubbornly.

She looks at him, understanding how deeply he is trapped inside their past. 'I know you don't,' she says.

She looks around desperately. The crowd has begun to thin as the morning's trading slows. She feels Shad's presence heavily beside her, the way she always has.

'Stay with the cart,' she tells him. 'I've got one more lot to buy.'

He nods obediently, beaming with relief.

She disappears into the crowd, leaving Shad far behind her, the way she used to as a child. She slips round the corner and hurries towards the river, where she knows that half a dozen sculls will be waiting for a penny fare. Even if he follows her across, by the time he reaches the other shore she'll have vanished once again. She thinks with dismay of her fruit and the cart she's left behind. The latter cost her two shillings and she will miss it, as it spared her arms the weight of the oranges on the long journey to Lambeth Walk.

She reaches the bank of the Thames and jumps into the first scull she sees. The pilot is an old woman, her heavily lined face ravaged by the weather, her grey hair caught back in a dirty kerchief. Her swollen fingers gripping the wooden oar handles, the old woman eases the scull back from the jetty in one swift movement, and the tiny boat shoots out into the Thames. She pulls the oars in long, perfectly judged movements and Nan is surprised by her vigour, for she appears as strong as any man. The tiny scull dodges larger boats and steamers as it makes its way across the river, their heavy wakes occasionally cresting the stern.

Nan stares down into the murky waters that surround her: sees her life lurking beneath the greenish scum. The river's stench is cut by the bitter December wind, but even so she pulls a handkerchief from the pocket of her dress and covers her nose. The old woman opposite her appears oblivious to the smell. She sucks in great draughts of air to fuel her strokes, but Nan can hear the rasping in the corners of her lungs.

When they are halfway across the river Nan spies Shad's figure on the bank, his hands thrust deep into the pockets of his trousers. He is not fool enough to follow, for he knows how quickly she will lose herself on the other side. He stands there watching. It is she who finally must turn away, unable to bear the sight of him another moment. She thought she'd lost him when he went to sea, that he was gone for good, either to the far side of the ocean, or underneath the waves, like his mam. Although the idea had eaten at her for a time, she'd made her peace with it. Now she feels as if the past has grabbed her by the throat.

She thinks fleetingly of her cart. It won't last half an hour in Houndsditch Market: some other girl will have it, glad to rid her arms of their burden. When the scull is a few yards from the shore, the old woman stops rowing and levels her flinty gaze at Nan. Nan fishes out the penny fare from her purse and hands it to her, and the woman drops it into the pocket of her skirt without so much as a nod. She reaches once again for the oars and heads for shore.

The tide is low and as they approach Nan can see three barefoot boys scamper across the mud flats, scavenging for lost coins and trinkets to sell. The scull grounds itself on the flats and Nan realises with dismay that she will have to dirty her feet in order to reach solid ground. She clambers over the side and steps gingerly into the mud, but as she does a bright red worm oozes out from underneath her shoe, its colour almost luminescent. She stops short, seeing another worm near the first and then another. She stares down at the blood-red worms just as the morning sun breaks through the haze. The mud glows red, and Nan feels as if she is stepping into fire.

23

Lulu

LULU SLIDES THE wadded cotton pads into the concealed pockets of his bustier and checks himself in the mirror. With a bit of rouge and powder he can heighten the effect. The muscles of his chest are already enlarged from the trapeze: it is but a little bit of artistry to transform the nature of their bulk. The French call it *trompe-l'oeil*, but Lulu likes to think of it as camouflage. His father, a master of sleight of hand, would turn in his grave if he could see his cleavage now.

Lulu prefers to think of his father as deceased, but in truth he has neither seen nor heard of him since he fled his homeland nearly a decade before. The old man could still be drawing crowds in the shady squares of Andalusia, for all he knows. Or perhaps he is old and crippled, unable to shuffle the cards the way he used to, or dance a jig on the rope with the fiddle tucked beneath his chin. Whatever his fate, Lulu has no wish to meet him on this earth.

But that does not lessen Lulu's debt. It was his father who

taught him how to walk the rope when he was still a tiny child, while his mother clutched a rosary to her breast with whitened knuckles. His father came from a long line of travelling showmen. Lulu remembers chance meetings on the road with brothers, uncles, cousins, long-lost friends. Without exception the men of his father's tribe bore the same stamp: they were short and barrel-chested with dark, bushy moustaches, expressive eyes and tempers that flashed too quickly in private. Entertainment was their birthright, and it seemed to Lulu that they had the ability to transform themselves at will, as long as an audience was near to hand.

His mother was more delicately wrought: a fragile woman whose expression was forever haunted by the folly of her marriage choice. She was not a traveller by birth, and the itinerant life did not agree with her. She rallied against it in her own quiet way, planting tiny seed-gardens everywhere they went, and painting the outside of the caravan to resemble the cottage she never had. As a child Lulu liked to pretend his mother had descended from a long line of royalty who would one day come in gilded carriages to claim them both. He had a birthmark on his thigh, which by some trick of fate nearly resembled a fleur-de-lis, lending credence to his fantasy. But while he owed his fine bone structure and delicate features to his mother, he owed his womanhood to his father.

It was he who first dressed Lulu in girl's clothes when he was only five, and persuaded his mother to curl his hair in long ringlets. Lulu had begun to perform at the age of four, but after a year his father decided that the act would be more sensational if he were a girl. Over the next eight years he gradually *became* one, until he no longer wore breeches between performances or even passed water in the company of other boys. His skill as a rope walker also increased, and he drew enormous crowds in every town they played. Like most performers he perfected a trademark stunt; his father christened it 'Lulu Ascending the Cross'. His father would stake a rope from the top of the church tower to a point on the ground some fifty metres distant. Lulu would tiptoe up the tautly stretched rope with a prayer book balanced on his head. Once atop the tower he would drape himself around the cross in the aspect of Christ's mourners in a sort of tableau vivant, a pose that never failed to win rapturous applause from the pious crowds down below. Finally, he would descend by one hand at a dizzying speed, his back arched, his toes pointed, his face thrown open to the heavens, hurtling earthwards like an angel straight into his father's arms. Father and daughter would embrace tenderly, and then Lulu would blush and curtsy and disappear into the caravan, leaving his father to fill his hat with offerings from the crowd, who felt themselves truly blessed to have witnessed such an act.

Lulu performed this stunt hundreds of times over a five-year period until one day, when he was nearly fifteen, his father found him in the embrace of an older boy behind the wagon. He ordered Lulu into the caravan and in a fit of rage pulled out his knife and cut the hair that had grown since childhood. Then, without a word, he hitched the horses to the wagon and they left that place, and Lulu's treasured curls, for ever.

When he woke at dawn the next morning it was to the

smell of his entire wardrobe smoking on the fire. His mother stitched some breeches and a shirt from an old theatrical curtain, and the following evening Lulu was reborn. But Luis the boy acrobat did not please the crowds so much as his predecessor, and after a year their earnings had dwindled so greatly that when his mother contracted brain fever they could not afford a physician. She died in Lulu's arms, and the day after she was buried Lulu fled his homeland and his father for good, stealing everything of value he could carry.

He travelled south to the ports and worked his passage on a ship bound for London. It was on board the *Santa Maria* that Lulu had his first real taste of men: of roughened cheeks and muscled arms and salty bursts of fluid. He knew at once that while he hated the incessant roll of the ocean and the perpetual unfurling of sails, sailors were something different altogether.

Lulu spent the entire voyage with two midshipmen, who agreed to receive him on alternate evenings, and by the time the ship docked in London he was convinced of his vocation. He sold his few remaining possessions, purchased a sequined bustier, a blond hairpiece and a cheap tiara, then got himself a theatrical agent. There was little work in London at the time, so he was forced to take a job in a regional circus in Birmingham, where he adopted the stage name of Mariah. It was in Birmingham that he discovered his facility for the flying trapeze, having only ever walked the tightrope for his father. The trapeze liberated him. Whereas the tightrope was all about discipline, balance and control, the trapeze was about speed and danger and the inexorable pull of gravity. But while he played to packed houses every evening, by day he was desperately lonely. He hated the narrow-minded provincialism of Birmingham and its residents. After six months he craved the anonymity of London, the hurly-burly of the streets, and the seedy cosmopolitanism of Leicester Square.

In desperation he turned to the Church for comfort, just as his mother had done before him. There he sought solace in a long line of choirboys until he was discovered and ejected rather unceremoniously from his post. The local press feasted on his downfall, running a series of interviews with the boys in question under the headline 'HAIL MARIAH!' Lulu was forced to leave town quickly in the dead of night. He returned to London, where his agent recommended a change of identity and a working sojourn abroad. He bought a brunette hairpiece and signed a two-year contract with a German circus touring the Continent. He adopted the stage name Calypso, and posed as a Mayan princess from South America who had learned the art of aerial flight on jungle vines. Once again he was a huge success, particularly in Bavaria and Austria, where men in lederhosen queued outside the stage door with gifts of bonbons and sweet wine. He deftly sidestepped them, preferring to seek out his own kind in the back alleys and waiting rooms of train stations. But after two years he tired of what had become an endless litany of one-night stands with soldiers and performers, and when his contract expired he returned to London.

Within a fortnight he'd signed a contract with Talliot's circus and had reassumed his former hair colour and identity. It was like stepping into a pair of comfortable old shoes. Lulu had been with him so long that he felt instantly relieved at the reunion. He cultivated a new circle of acquaintances in the gentlemen's clubs behind Tottenham Court Road, where he quickly discovered that he was not alone in his penchant for female dress. Through this same circle he acquired respectable rooms in Bloomsbury from a sympathetic landlord. This time, however, he was careful not to confuse his public and private personae. He did not wish to repeat his mistakes with the Birmingham press, and guarded his professional identity with care. He took a series of lovers of different backgrounds and nationalities, and even found himself the object of intense attention from an English lord for a time. But he was lonely. Until he met Nan, he could not number among his acquaintances in London a single friend.

Sex had always marred his previous attempts at friendship. He did not have this problem with Nan. In truth he was a little bit in love with her, the way one might idolise an older sister. In Lulu's eyes, Nan was everything he was not: practical, unassuming, effortlessly beautiful, and female. That she'd suffered poverty, a failed affair, and the death of a child only heightened her allure and lent her a sort of tragic dignity. Apart from the passing of his mother, Lulu had never experienced anything so momentous. His own life was a long series of daredevil feats, risqué sexual episodes, and brief interludes of notoriety. It lacked substance and gravitas; moreover, it lacked suffering. Lulu felt this acutely in her presence: that Nan's life was real in a way that his was not, even if that reality was sometimes unpleasant. Lulu had spent his entire life in an elaborate fantasy land of his own creation, a land of silk and sequins, stolen kisses in the backs of hansom cabs, rapturous applause and the exhilarating flight of angels.

What would happen when he grew too old to fly? Who would applaud or kiss him when he lost his youth?

He stares at his reflection in the mirror and, not for the first time, feels a shiver of apprehension. Then he hears a scrabbling just outside, and turns to see Nan in the doorway, her face ghostlike, her long hair slick with rain. Her expression is pained. In an instant he is reminded of the night he first found her. There is something else that strikes him as odd but it takes a moment for him to realise what it is. And then he sees that she is empty-handed.

24

Nan

THE DAY SHAD returns from Plymouth is scratched hard into her memory.

For two weeks the weather has been hot and densely humid. It buckles her knees and thickens her brain. One morning she oversleeps, and when she wakes, the sheet beneath her head is damp with sweat. By the time she arrives in Houndsditch, the day's oranges have almost gone. Only one vendor remains. She picks up a piece of fruit and gives it a squeeze, and her fingertips leave a dull impression on the rind, like hammered tin. The vendor scowls at her, and Nan drops the orange back into the basket. She turns her back on him and drifts away.

Instead she heads south, to the river, and finds a seat upon an iron bench not far from where her father disappeared. Already the sky over the Thames glowers with humidity. She likes to think of him still there, tinkering with his hoe just beneath the water's surface, as if at any moment he will burst forth like a fountain, clutching his hat in one hand and a silver teapot in the other. She would like to spend the morning here, but after a short time she is defeated by the river's stench.

She wanders past Custom House Quay, turning away from the river just before she reaches the rail terminal at Cannon Street. Her life has meandered since her father's death. She works twice as many hours as before, partly because she needs the earnings, partly to fill the gap left by his absence. For a while she let herself be courted. The boy was a coster whom she'd known briefly in her year at school. She walked out with him for a time, but when he began to speak of love, she shed him. Nan does not trust the idea of love. She has no proof that it exists.

Eventually she finds herself at St Paul's. She climbs the marble steps and creeps inside the cool darkness, choosing a quiet pew at the back. She watches as a steady stream of tourists wander by, wiping at the perspiration on their brows, their eyes glazed with fatigue. She listens to a choir of boys rehearsing, closes her eyes and lets their crisp, high voices seep into her. She dozes off, and when she wakes the choir is gone. She looks around and sees the church is empty. She creeps out from her place only when they begin to shut the outer doors. The verger looks at her with startled eyes, as if she is an apparition. She waves to him, slipping through the opening without a word, and stands at the top of the white stone steps, blinking in the hazy summer light.

Her eyes come to rest on Shad. He is standing at the

bottom of the steps staring up at her with a look of perfect seriousness. She recognises him instantly, though she has not seen him in nine years. He is no longer a boy, but he does not have the congealed look of a man.

He is surrounded by pigeons. When one hops upon his head, she realises he's been feeding them. He flinches when he sees her, brushing the bird aside with one arm, then slowly climbs the steps to where she stands. She feels a sudden rush of longing for the past. Shad pauses on the step just below hers.

'I found you,' he says, as if she has been hiding from him all these years in some elaborate game of hide-and-seek.

'Hello, Shad.' She reaches out a hand to touch the scar on his forehead, the one she gave him as a keepsake. Shad frowns at her, exactly the way he used to as a boy, and she cannot help but laugh. She throws her arms about his neck and pulls him into an embrace, whispering into the brown of his neck, 'You can't be cross with me after all this time.' She feels him take a deep breath, sees his arms hanging stiffly in the air, like a puppet's. Then they settle lightly round her waist, and slowly tighten like a knot.

He tells her he has been in London less than a fortnight. She can see that he is lost in the city now, and no longer understands its ways. She finds him a room near her own, using her small savings to pay the first week's rent, for he has come to London almost empty-handed.

'What of your father?' she asks.

He shrugs. 'Dead.'

She smiles, and links her arm through his. 'Then we are both orphans.'

He stops short and looks at her. 'Except that we are grown,' he says.

She shows him how to find work at the docks. He is tall and lean and muscled, and is chosen quickly from the long line of men who arrive each morning. Some days there is no work, so he helps her with the oranges. Nan sees the glances from the others, for he is smooth-faced and olive-skinned, and his curly hair is the colour of caramel. On Sundays they walk out together, to Regent's Park or Vauxhall Gardens, or go by train to Crystal Palace.

One Saturday night Shad takes her to the Alhambra. He has seen a poster of Ada Mencken as Marzeppa, strapped across the back of a white stallion. In the poster she appears naked, though on the night of the performance she wears a flesh-coloured stocking from head to toe. The illusion works, however. Throughout the evening Shad watches silently, his lips slightly parted. Never once does he take his eyes from the stage. Nan watches him covertly, and is surprised to feel the slow burn of jealousy.

When winter comes, the weather freezes. There are strikes at the docks; the price of fruit soars, and for the first time Nan cannot afford to trade. Shad is turned out of his room, and he and Nan are forced to seek cheaper accommodation elsewhere. They find a tiny room to share on the outskirts of St Giles' Rookery.

On their first night, Nan looks about the room and smiles.

'It's like the one we shared as children. Before Fleur was born.'

'But we aren't children any longer,' he says. Then he takes a step forward and does what he has meant to do all along. Nan is too stunned at first to protest but, after a few moments, she forgets herself entirely. She can think only of the tight feel of Shad in her arms.

25

Nathan

TWO HOURS BEFORE showtime, Nathan goes in search of Talliot. The orang-utan has not touched her food in three days, and Nathan has begun to fear that something is amiss. He does not know what Talliot can do, but he does not want the burden of the animal's care on his shoulders alone.

The main tent is empty so he goes backstage to the area where the props and costumes are kept. Two of the equestri-ennes are lying on an old mattress in the corner, reading a penny broadsheet. They are twins and share the same heavy features: bulging eyes, thick lips and meaty jowls. Nathan has never spoken to them in the past; they speak only to their horses or each other, and he has given them a wide berth since he came. Already they have rouged each other's faces, though they have yet to put on their buckskin costumes. They wear only riding breeches and loose tunics and when Nathan stops to address them, they behave as if he is speaking in tongues. 'Talliot,' he repeats, in response to their mute stares.

One of them shrugs and shakes her head.

Nathan hears voices, and turns towards Lulu's dressing room. He hesitates at the open doorway, just as Lulu embraces Nan. They turn to look at him with startled faces, and once again Nathan feels an outsider. He sees that Nan has been crying; at the sight of him she wipes a stray tear from her cheek with her hand. His eyes flicker over Lulu's sequined bustier; he cannot help himself. Lulu pulls back from Nan and straightens, throwing back his shoulders. Nathan feels his face redden.

He mumbles an apology and hurries away, confused by the sight of their embrace. Their friendship is no secret, but for the first time it occurs to him that he knows nothing of its nature.

As he re-enters the menagerie tent, he remembers Kezia. He goes to the orang-utan's cage and opens the door slowly, crouching down so as not to give the animal fright. He can see her hiding behind straw in her box, her dark eyes shining in the reflection of the gaslight. A pile of rotting fruit and vegetables sits untouched in the corner of the cage; it is yesterday's ration and has turned brown overnight, though that has not discouraged the houseflies. Nathan scoops up the pile with a shovel and dumps it in the gutter. Let the rats feast upon it if Kezia will not, he thinks. He cuts up a half-ration of new fruit and puts it in the same spot, though he knows his effort will be wasted.

He stares at her in silence, hoping to convey some sympathy through the metal bars. When he finally looks away, the Skeleton Man is standing quietly in the shadows behind him. Nathan gives a start. He points to the cage.

'She won't eat.'

The Skeleton Man moves forward out of the shadows to where Nathan stands. They both regard the box in the corner of the cage.

'Perhaps she isn't hungry.'

'She will starve,' says Nathan hopelessly.

'Maybe that is her objective,' says the Skeleton Man with equanimity.

Nathan frowns.

The Skeleton Man raises a bony arm and indicates the menagerie tent. 'There will come a time when all of us will wish to be set free.'

'I would not choose to die,' says Nathan fervently.

The Skeleton Man smiles. 'Why?' he asks simply. 'Is this life so very good? Or is death so very evil?'

Nathan hesitates. He feels that the question has been phrased deliberately as a trick. However, the Skeleton Man's expression is benign.

The Skeleton Man shuffles forward to the cage and calls softly to Kezia. He repeats her name over and over, his voice no more than a whisper. After a minute, Nathan sees the animal stir in her box, and hears the rustle of the straw. She does not emerge from the box, but eventually she pokes her head out of the shadows to meet the Skeleton Man's gaze.

He stops chanting her name, having achieved his own mysterious purpose. 'We should leave her,' he says decisively.

Nathan nods, inwardly relieved, as if the Skeleton Man has absorbed his responsibility.

The Skeleton Man walks slowly to the bar and pours himself a cup of tea. Even the tiny weight of the metal teapot strains the wasted muscle of his arm. He glances up, and catches Nathan's stare.

'What is it?' he asks.

Nathan colours and shakes his head.

The Skeleton Man cocks his head. 'You've a question on your lips. Ask it.'

'The pot in your hands,' Nathan stammers. 'I just wondered for a moment, what it must feel like . . .' his voice tails off.

'To be me?'

Nathan nods.

He chooses his words with care. 'Sometimes, on a good day, it feels like nothing at all. The pot is there and I can lift it, and that is a blessing. Other times, it is not so simple . . . it is like scaling a mountain that never ends. One must simply continue, because there is no alternative.'

'But you could eat,' says Nathan earnestly. 'Just like Kezia.'

He smiles a little ruefully and shakes his head from side to side. The smile slowly disappears. 'It used to be my family who were starving,' he says finally. 'Now it is only me.'

Nathan frowns, unable to understand why a man possessed of so much wisdom should seek to starve in order to survive. He does not know how to pose this question.

The Skeleton Man shrugs. 'Besides, my life is not so very hard. My wife and children are well and we have managed to remain together. They are all that matters.'

'But what if you fall ill?' says Nathan. Or die, he thinks.

'I won't,' says the Skeleton Man unequivocally.

'But is there no alternative? Could you not find some other means?' he asks.

'It is too late,' says the Skeleton Man simply. His voice is empty of bitterness or regret. 'It is too late for alternatives.'

Nathan does not know what to feel. The Skeleton Man leans forward and lays a hand on his arm. Nathan can feel the strength in his grip, and the effort such an action costs him.

'There is no *thing* on this earth worthy of our sacrifice,' he says intently. 'There are only people – individuals for whom we should risk everything, if necessary. Anyone who claims otherwise is a liar or a fool.'

Nathan nods, but the words weigh heavily upon him.

26

Nan

NAN WAITS FOR Lulu in the cold light of dawn on London Bridge. He has promised to accompany her to Houndsditch Market, to see if she can recover her cart. She does not wish to go alone, for she feels certain that Shad will wait for her again this morning. He knows that she has nothing but her oranges – that without them she would not survive. She should not have fled from him, for she will only have to face him in the end, and make peace with her own history. This morning, at least, she will have Lulu by her side: proof that her life is not unchanged. A man, of sorts, she thinks with a smile. Well, half a man.

Although the sky is lit by only a finger of light, the bridge is already packed. Below her, the boats have begun to stir like giant insects upon the water. She stares down at the muddy swirl of current and sees an empty bottle spinning lazily in the drift, its cork still intact. She thinks of the first time she spoke to Nathan: one day she came upon him here by accident, not long after he'd joined the circus. He sat astride the parapet the way one would a horse, and she was struck by how odd he looked, how out of place and time. He stared down at the Thames, and when she stopped and spoke to him, he appeared at first not to recognise her.

'What are you doing?' she asked. Her tone was innocent, a polite attempt at conversation.

Nathan hesitated, as if he was reluctant to answer. 'We don't have rivers like this where I come from,' he said finally.

'What *do* you have?' she asked.

'Plains. Grass. Oceans of it. As far as you can see.'

Nan frowned. She could not imagine this. 'Is that all?'

The boy shrugged. 'There are towns. Made of wood, not bricks. And the streets are full of mud.' He looked at Nan a little tentatively and she smiled to encourage him.

'What else?'

The boy paused again, but this time she could tell that he was thinking. 'In summer, it is so hot you can fry an egg without a fire,' he said finally. 'In winter, the snow falls higher than a horse.'

Nan looked at him doubtfully. Was he making fun of her?

The boy continued, 'And if you lick your lips, they will freeze shut. Like this.' He demonstrated, pressing his lips together in a thin line. Nan could not help but laugh. The boy smiled at her then. Then he looked back down at the river, as if he could not keep his eyes from it for long.

'But we have no river like the Thames,' he said after a moment. Nan looked at him and his eyes were suddenly serious, scanning the river's surface. 'This one is alive.'

He stared out at the water, and Nan grew suddenly self-conscious, as if her presence was an interruption. She wished that she could see it through his eyes. To her, the Thames would always be the same: deep and wide and full of death.

He must have sensed her unease, for he coughed and looked sideways at her. Embarrassed, she excused herself, and the boy nodded goodbye, turning to watch her as she walked across the bridge. She regretted she'd not had the courage to join him that day, although he hadn't asked her.

Now she looks into the deep brown water and can think only of the expression on his face yesterday outside Lulu's dressing room. Although it was he who mistook her embrace with Lulu, she feels tainted by it.

She feels a tap on her shoulder and turns to see Lulu standing there, freshly washed and shaved. He wears the dress of a gentleman: top hat and long frock coat, and carries a walking stick in his hand. She bursts out laughing.

Lulu holds out his arms. 'Am I not acceptable?'

She links her arm through his. 'Of course you are.'

'You weren't expecting me to wear a gown?'

'Don't be daft.'

'I must make an impression.'

Nan considers this. Lulu is right: Shad has always been intimidated by the well-to-do. She pulls Lulu along through the crowd. 'I'll be the laughing stock of Houndsditch,' she murmurs with a smile. 'They'll wonder why I still sell oranges if I'm with the likes of you.'

'Because I like oranges,' says Lulu confidently. 'I will tell them so.'

'I think you'd best let me do the talking,' says Nan.

Two hours later, they have searched the entire market but have found nothing of Nan's cart. She asks among the traders and other orange girls, but no one admits to having seen it. Each time she turns round, she thinks Shad will be standing there. She cannot believe he hasn't come. His absence irritates her. She had been certain he would try to speak with her again.

Lulu, however, is relieved. 'Come,' he says, pulling lightly on her arm. 'Let's go and have some breakfast.' Nan frowns but finally agrees. It is not the cart that worries her. She has set aside some money and can afford to buy another. It is her failure to confront the past: without Shad she cannot do so.

27

Nathan

NATHAN HOVERS BEHIND the back row under cover of darkness. From there he can see everything, but is invisible to those performing. The house is full tonight and the audience is a lively one: they cheer and catcall and burst into laughter at the slightest provocation, as if they are determined to be entertained. When Lulu skips into the ring they whistle and stamp their feet wildly, and Nathan wonders for a moment what it must feel like to be the object of so much desire.

His own experience in the ring cannot compare. When Nathan performs he is conscious of the crowd's admiration, and occasionally of their envy. Simply by stepping into the ring he achieves this. He can feel the crowd's attention transform him: it swells his stature and importance. However, he has no illusions about the nature of their interest. It is the lions that excite them, not him, and it is the possibility of a mauling that stirs them most.

With Lulu it is different. Lulu *is* the spectacle, and he

carries the crowd along with him easily. Nathan watches Lulu climb the rope to the trapeze and settle on it like a child does a swing. He leans back, kicking his legs out, and pulls hard on the ropes, building up momentum as he moves across the ceiling. Nathan waits with the others for Lulu to make his first manoeuvre, and as always feels his body tense with anticipation. Then he is distracted by a stirring just behind him. He glances over his shoulder in the darkness, where a young man much taller than himself has squeezed into the gap. Nathan shuffles forward and turns his head again, for something about the man's appearance snags his memory. He has seen this man before, recognises the closely shorn treacle-coloured hair, the long, thin face and full lips. And then he realises that the man behind him is the sailor who danced with Nan in the New Cut.

Nathan eases himself further sideways so he can get a better look. Up close the sailor is much younger than he'd thought, and bristling with the nervous energy of youth. He stares intently at Lulu, but not with lust or admiration or even pleasure. As Lulu goes through his routine, the sailor does not gasp or clap or smile, but merely follows every movement with his eyes. Lulu's performance is perfectly executed: with each trick the audience almost heaves with relief, but the sailor's face registers nothing. Not until the last moment, when Lulu takes his bow and Nan steps forward into the ring and tosses him an orange, does Nathan see a flicker of response. For the first time, the sailor's face tightens. Nathan is so close that he can see the clenching of his jaw. The sailor's eyes sweep from Lulu to Nan, and watch even more intently as she smiles and waves to the crowd, who respond with a good-natured cheer. Nan seems radiant in the limelight, as if she too is transformed by it, and Nathan cannot take his eyes from her. Finally he turns to see the sailor frowning in the darkness. Nathan wonders whether Nan is aware of his presence, although she does not glance in their direction. Suddenly, while the crowd is still rapturous with applause, the sailor turns and brushes past him, so close that Nathan can smell him. He watches as the sailor hurries down the steps and disappears out of the rear exit.

Nathan looks for Nan in the crowd below him. Her oranges are in demand now, and she banters easily with the men who queue to buy from her disappearing stock. Oranges are a man's fruit, he thinks with dismay. He watches Nan brush a stray whisp of hair back from her face. What man would not want her?

Twenty minutes later Nathan himself is in the ring. He has forgotten about Nan and the sailor, and thinks only of the animals in front of him. The lions are uneasy this evening; an angry skirmish broke out only minutes before showtime. Nathan does not know what brought it on, only that Nero nurses a small tear to his shoulder as a consequence. Nero is in no mood to perform and with every movement signals this to Nathan, the hairs along his spine bristling with displeasure. Nathan must work twice as hard, using every ounce of concentration to control him. Within half a minute of entering the ring, he can feel the sweat trickling down his sides.

Despite this, the first minutes of the act pass smoothly. The lions seat themselves on their pedestals and rear up on their haunches, roaring in unison. Nathan barks a series of commands at them and they climb down from the pedestals and leap from a line of perches he has placed at five-foot intervals. Queen performs willing enough, but twice Nero hesitates and snarls at him before continuing with the act. When he is finished, Nathan instructs them to lie down and roll over, a trick he has mastered just a few days before. They do so perfectly, and Nathan gives an inward sigh of relief.

For the first time he hears the noise of the audience, and turns towards their applause. He raises his arms to the crowd with a flourish: more and more he has learned to be the showman, though it does not come easily. Then, as his eyes sweep across the crowd, they alight on Nan. She is standing to one side, the tray of oranges in her hand, and Nathan ceases to hear sound. He thinks of the sailor, remembers their embrace, and wonders what her lips would feel like upon his. Nan smiles at him, a little tentatively at first, and Nathan feels a tightening in his throat. He pauses, forgetting himself, until Nan looks down with an embarrassed laugh and he forces his gaze away.

He turns back to Queen and Nero and gives the next command, but his mind is still with Nan on the far side of the ring. Queen obeys his signal, rising and trotting to her mark at the other end of the cage, but Nero does not. Nathan looks at him and once again forgets his purpose. He sees only a lion, as if he is in the cage for the first time. Nero senses his distraction and something else, perhaps his fear, and rushes him, closing the distance between them in a few short bounds. Nathan sees it all in slow motion, as if in a dream. Nero's enormous paw comes at him with claws outstretched, and he feels a searing in his arm. He cracks the whip down hard in Nero's direction. The noise is deafening, but its impact is immediate, for Nero stops short with surprise. Nathan cracks the whip again and shouts at him to follow Queen. Nathan is suddenly tired of Nero's sulky moods and violent temper, and angry that the lion is not worthy of his trust. Nero retreats to the far end of the cage and Nathan finishes the act as quickly as he can. The crowd is fired with excitement and the applause is thunderous; Nathan has never heard it so loud, and the fact irritates him. As he winds up the act, he feels only rage at Nero and scorn for those watching. He ushers the animals back to the menagerie tent and then looks down and sees the blood massing on his arm. The sight explains the crowd's delirium, but it repels him.

The Skeleton Man is behind him, staring at his wounded arm. Nathan is still shaking with anger, but the Skeleton Man steers him across the tent to the bar, where Walter is already setting out a large glass of brandy.

'Drink this,' says the Skeleton Man, handing him the glass. Nathan feels the liquid burn his insides, meshing with the searing pain in his arm. The Skeleton Man gingerly lifts his arm and the three men together examine the wound: not deep, but long, the blood already beginning to congeal in several spots. 'We must clean it right away,' says the Skeleton Man. He douses it with brandy and then tears a strip of cloth from a clean rag with his teeth, binding the wound quickly. Nathan watches him work, amazed at his efficiency; he would not have guessed that he was capable of such action.

'What happened out there?' asks the Skeleton Man. His tone is deliberately calm, almost conversational. Nathan realises that he does not wish to alarm him. He takes a deep breath and shakes his head.

'I don't know,' he says, for at that moment his mind is truly blank. Walter sets another glass of brandy on the counter and, as Nathan reaches for it, he sees the tremor in his good hand. Although he tries he cannot quell the shaking.

Then he remembers Nan: sees her smile flash before him in the ring. He turns to the Skeleton Man. 'I lost my concentration for a moment,' he says absently.

'You're lucky it was only that,' he replies with a smile. Both men turn and watch the lions. Nero lies in the corner of the cage feigning sleep, while Queen cleans herself obsessively with a paw.

Talliot rushes in, his face concerned. 'Are you all right?' he says, but even as Nathan starts to answer, Talliot's attention strays towards the cage. 'He isn't fit for dog meat!' he says, shaking his head with disgust. Nero opens one eye, but does not move, as if Talliot's outburst does not warrant a response.

'It wasn't his fault,' says Nathan. 'I gave the wrong signal. He got confused.' The Skeleton Man glances up sharply at Nathan but says nothing. Talliot looks at Nathan, and shrugs.

'Then learn your lines,' he says with a grunt, and stalks out of the tent.

The Skeleton Man turns to Nathan and raises an eyebrow. 'You didn't give the wrong signal,' he remarks, a trace of amusement in his eyes.

'I could have.'

The Skeleton Man gingerly pours himself a cup of tea, while Nathan sips at his brandy, and Walter rubs his stump, eyeing Nathan's wounded arm. They sit in silence, punctuated only by the sound of hoofs and the occasional roaring of the crowd, for the equestrienne twins are now halfway through their act. Nathan thinks of Nan and her smile. He does not trust his memory, and wonders whether he imagined it. He feels a fool. Then he hears a noise behind him, and turns to see his mother in her chair.

She looks at him icily. 'Your performance was careless,' she says in clipped tones. 'You are only alive because he chose not to kill you. I trust you realise this.'

Nathan is speechless. His eyes drift down to the glass of brandy still clutched in his good hand.

'You must clean the wound every hour,' she continues. 'If you do not, it will turn septic, and you will die before the week is out. It is not a pleasant way to go, I promise you.' She turns her wheelchair round as if to leave, then pauses briefly, speaking over her shoulder. 'And, Nathan,' she says sharply, 'if you cannot keep your mind on the act, then you have no business being in the ring.' She pauses then to let her meaning crystallise. 'Is that understood?'

Nathan feels his face redden. He is grateful that her back is turned. 'Yes,' he answers, his voice cracking.

28

Nathan

NATHAN HAS ANOTHER memory of her, but this one he has tried to forget. In it, he wakes early one morning to find his mother in an ill-fitting suit of sombre grey that he has never seen before. The clothes are like a warning. He knows they are important, but does not know why. Several times over breakfast he shuts his eyes tightly, hoping that when he opens them his mother will be dressed in the buckskin breeches he is used to, but his efforts do not work. He scowls into his food.

All his life they have moved from place to place. The terrain outside the wagon has altered constantly. He has grown used to this, has even welcomed its diversion at times, but other sorts of change he cannot tolerate. He wants his life within the wagon to stay the same.

While he eats, his mother does not join him as usual. Instead she carefully pins up her hair, then goes and sits upon the wooden steps at the wagon's rear. When he is finished, he jumps past her to the grass below, and sees something wedged into the wagon's canvas by her side. He stops and stares at it: a small leather suitcase he has never seen before. Like the suit it has appeared, miraculously, during the night. His mother does not notice his stare. She is distracted this morning, has barely spoken since he woke, and does not listen when he speaks.

Instead she sits quietly, eyes ahead, smoking cigarettes she rolls herself from a tiny sheaf of whisper-thin paper. Nathan skips about the grass, the morning dew wetting his bare legs, while his mother smokes one cigarette after another. Eventually he tires of playing, and clambers up into the wagon, planting himself on the step beside her. She inches her hips a little to one side to make room for him, and he takes this as a good sign, a sign that she remembers him, is perhaps pleased to have him with her. Already the day is hot and windless. The smoke from her cigarette drifts into his eyes. His mother does not notice, even when he rubs them with the palms of his hands. He sees her shoo a fly that is buzzing round her head with a wave of one hand. They sit in silence for a while, until her cigarette is finished. She stubs it out on the side of the wagon and he watches as it arcs through the air on to the grass below, where it continues to smoulder. He has an urge to go and fetch it, hold it in his hand before the heat disappears, but he does not wish to leave his place beside his mother.

They sit for an eternity. He does not know how long, nor what exactly they are waiting for, but he knows that she is waiting. He wonders why she does not go to check upon her horses; wonders who will feed and brush them, and exercise them in the ring. However, he does not speak of horses. He is grateful that for once she chooses him instead of them.

They have risen earlier than usual, and he watches as the other members of the troupe come to life around them. He sees Riza emerge from his wagon, blinking in the morning sun. The strongman nods and smiles at him, and Nathan eagerly waves back. He watches as Riza crosses over to the well and begins to pump water, the muscles on his arms rippling inside his skin like eels. Riza splashes water on his face and over his head for several moments, and when he finally straightens the water runs in tiny rivulets down his gleaming chest. He stops and stares at them, and this time does not smile. Then Nathan sees that Riza does not look at him, but at his mother, at her grey wool suit and pinned-up hair, and the absence of expression in her eyes, as if she is already somewhere else. Even from a distance Nathan can see Riza's eyes darken, and a furrowed line travel across his brow. His mother sees nothing, does not even glance in the direction of the strongman. Finally, Riza tears his eyes away and lumbers slowly across the grass to the main tent, where he disappears inside. Nathan has an urge to run across the grass and feel the strongman lift him high into the air.

But he does nothing. Instead he closes his eyes and concentrates on the feel of his mother beside him. He can sense the warmth of her through the clothes he does not like, can even smell their newness, intermixed with her own peculiar musky scent. After a time he opens his eyes and begins to swing his legs lightly underneath him, causing the wooden plank they sit upon to shudder slightly with the movement. His mother lays a warm hand upon his thigh; with the tiniest bit of pressure she communicates her desire that he should stop. He does, instantly. She leaves her hand upon his leg, and he stares down at her long slender fingers, marvelling at the perfect crescent moons upon her nails. Her hands are beautiful, he thinks. He wishes they were his.

Later, he dozes off in the mid-morning sun, his head lolling gently on her lap. He sleeps deeply, and dreams of horses in the ring, tiny horses no taller than his knee. The horses circle endlessly around him. His mother has left him in the ring, has put him on the pedestal without a word, and now he can only watch as the tiny horses whinny, toss their heads and kick their feet with restless energy. He has the feeling that he cannot move, that if he does they will come at him instead, so he sits quietly, waiting for the show to end.

When he wakes, he feels the hard wooden plank against the side of his head. He sits up, rubbing his ear. The sun is high overhead, and his mouth is parched from the heat. All around him the camp is quiet. His mother and her suitcase are gone.

29

Nan

NAN HURRIES ALONG the darkened street that leads to her place of lodging. It is a respectable boarding house for women only, the best she's managed since her father died, and a relief after the squalid life of the rookery. But secretly she feels an impostor, as if the words *dead child* have been burned across her back. She comes and goes quietly, and keeps her distance from the others.

She shares a room with a girl of nineteen called Charlotte, and one of twenty-one called Martha. They've come to London from the provinces, but they've quickly gleaned the ways of the city. Both work as trouser-stitchers in Savile Row, and while they complain about the hours and the pay, Nan knows they prefer it to the dismal life of servants. Martha is tall and broad and rakish-looking, while Charlotte is thin and elfin-faced. Nan wishes they were stupid: dairy maids with sheep eyes and dazed smiles, come to London in search of husbands. But they are sharp-eyed and quick-tongued, and there is something ruthless about their friendship. From the first day they have preyed on her, scrutinising her every move, and probing her for details of her past. Once, when she revealed that she'd lived briefly in the rookery, they asked her outright whether she'd been on the game.

Tonight, when she opens the door, they sit facing each other upon the bed playing cards. They look up when she enters, the older one, Martha, manages a nod of greeting. Nan goes to her bed and removes her coat. There, beside her bed, is the orange cart.

'You had a visitor,' says Martha archly. Both girls watch her.

Nan says nothing. She wonders what Shad has told them, but cannot bring herself to ask. She stares down at the empty cart. Where are her oranges?

'A sailor,' continues Martha. 'He found your cart.' She sweeps up the cards and begins to shuffle them. 'Do you know him?'

Nan hesitates. 'No,' she says, turning her back on them. She takes up a small ivory-handled hairbrush that belonged to her mother, and begins to pull at her hair in long strokes. Shad must have known that she was out when he came, for it is just the sort of needling trick that he would pull.

'That's funny. He knew all about you,' says Martha coolly.

Nan stops brushing. She can feel the weight of their eyes upon her. She knows that Shad will stop at nothing to reclaim her, and wonders desperately what he has told them. It is almost more than she can bear. Nan feels her face grow hot, and sees the ivory-handled brush begin to swim before her eyes, but she'll not be goaded into revelations by these two.

She takes up her coat and bag and goes to the door, leaving the two girls wide-eyed behind her.

Once outside, she pauses in the cold night air to regain herself. She will have to finish with Shad for good; she knows that now. She will spend the night at Lulu's, and hunt him out tomorrow. She hurries along the road and reaches Bloomsbury in less than half an hour. It is late and the area is quiet, except for the occasional hansom rattling by. Nan arrives at Lulu's flat and knocks upon the door, but there is silence.

With relief, she sees a cab round the corner. It stops so close that she can almost feel the hot breath of the horses. But when the door opens, a well-dressed man with silver hair emerges, followed by a much younger woman. The man pays off the driver, then offers the woman his arm. They turn and pass within a few feet of Nan on their way to the flat next door, and with a sweeping, hostile glance the young woman's gaze meets hers. She is hardly more than a girl. She wears a dark red gown and a cheap brown stole thrown loosely round her shoulders. Her blonde hair is in disarray, as if the evening's entertainment has already begun.

Nan has no choice but to leave. She knows that Lulu often stays out until dawn, though she does not know where. She thinks of returning to her room, but cannot bring herself to do so. Instead she heads south towards the river. She will spend the night at the circus if she must.

The journey takes her nearly an hour and, by the time she reaches Lambeth Walk, it is past midnight and her entire body aches with tiredness. The entrance to the tent is locked, but she squeezes through a tiny rent in the canvas at the back. Inside the tent is pitch-black, and she realises with dismay that it is bone-chillingly cold. She did not know what she'd expected – perhaps some vestige of heat from the hundreds of bodies who had warmed the space hours before. But there is nothing to suggest a human presence in the place, only the smell of sawdust, horse manure, and orange peel underfoot.

She feels her way out into the centre of the ring, a place she has never been before, and turns slowly round, her eyes gradually adjusting to the darkness. She shuts her eyes and tries to imagine the tent as it was earlier, the bright lights upon her and the gaze of the crowd but the tent is so deathly still that panic rises up in her. She hears a low rumbling, muffled by canvas and distance, and almost does not recognise the lion's roar. She heads towards the passageway that leads to the menagerie, hoping that it will be warmer there. She will not have to pass the night with only the spectre of an audience for company.

As she approaches the door to the menagerie, Nan is relieved to see a faint shaft of light from within. As she suspected, the iron stove is lit, and this tent is much warmer than the other. However, she is surprised to see a small paraffin lamp still lit on the bar. She goes to the stove to warm her hands. Most of the animals are hidden in the half-darkness, though she can hear the occasional rustling of straw. Only Queen and Nero are visible, and she sees with a start that they are not alone.

Nathan lies asleep upon a bedroll just behind the lion cage. He is on his back, head lolling to one side, one arm thrown out at an angle. The smooth skin of his face glows golden in the lamplight. Nan is instantly embarrassed. The only man she has ever seen asleep is Shad. She knows that she should leave at once. Instead she inches carefully towards him, stopping only a few feet from where he lies. She can hear the faint sound of his breath. At least he is clothed, she thinks, though he has loosened the top buttons on his shirtfront and she can see the pale triangle of skin at his chest. She sinks slowly to her knees and leans in close, studies the jagged fall of his parting and the way the hair fans across his face. Her eyes come to rest on the small shadow of indentation at the back of his neck, where she imagines tracing the tiny crevice with the tips of her fingers.

Behind her, Queen rises and gives a short snarl. Nathan stirs. Nan jumps to her feet, but it is too late: Nathan rises up on one elbow and peers at her sleepily.

'Hullo.'

'I'm sorry,' she stammers. 'I didn't know you were here.'

He sits up and rubs his palm across his face. 'It doesn't matter.' He stands, and they stare at each other awkwardly.

'Do you sleep here?' she asks.

'Sometimes.'

'Why?'

He shrugs. 'I like it here.'

'Does Talliot know?'

'Maybe. I don't know.' The thought does not seem to worry him. 'What are you doing here?'

Nan hesitates. 'There was some trouble at my lodging house,' she says finally. 'I needed somewhere to go.'

'You look cold.' He crosses the room and slips behind the

long wooden bar, pulling out a large bottle of brandy. He pours some into a glass, then carries it back to her. 'Here. Drink this.'

She takes a large sip while he watches. She does not know if it is the brandy or the fact that Nathan is staring at her, but her insides start to glow. She smiles at him, and is surprised to see him flush. He steps backwards.

Nero raises himself to a sitting position and gives a short bark of a roar, as if he wants to be noticed. Nan walks slowly towards the cage.

'He's the one who clawed you.'

Nathan frowns. 'He was upset.'

Nan glances at him with surprise.

'Besides, it wasn't me he wanted.'

'What do you mean?' she asks.

'It's Queen,' says Nathan. 'For Nero, it's always about Queen.'

She frowns. 'What of her?' They both look at Queen, who remains stretched out, though Nan can see that she's awake.

Nathan pauses. 'Queen's alone,' he says. His voice carries the faintest whisper of regret.

'But she's expecting,' says Nan.

Nathan shakes his head. 'It isn't the same.' He looks right at her, and Nan feels as if her past has been exposed.

Nathan crosses to the door of the cage, unlocking it. 'You can come in if you like,' he says casually.

She looks at him askance, but sees that he is serious.

'All right,' she hears herself reply. He holds the door open for her. As if on cue, Queen and Nero both turn to gaze unblinking at her. She freezes. The three of them watch her expectantly, and Nan feels herself rooted to the floor.

'Is it safe?' she asks nervously.

'It is with me here.'

She hopes he is right. He pushes the heavy iron door inwards, and they both step inside. She hears him draw the bolt behind her, but by then she is already trapped in the tawny glow of Nero's gaze. Nathan walks slowly over to the lion. Nan flashes him a nervous smile. Her heart is racing and she feels a little giddy, as if she is swimming in Moselle.

'He's watching me,' she says.

'Why shouldn't he? You're in his cage.'

'I could leave,' says Nan quickly.

'He's just curious. Come closer. Let him get the scent of you.'

Nan takes a deep breath. The words settle in her brain uncomfortably, perhaps because she was not aware she had a scent, but as she steps closer she realises that it is Nero whose scent is overpowering. She inches forward until the acrid heat of him seems to surround and penetrate her. She is so close that she could touch him.

'That's better,' says Nathan.

Nan's eyes stray to the wound on Nathan's arm. 'Do you trust him?' she asks.

Nathan hesitates. 'It's Queen I trust,' he says. He goes to Queen and kneels down by her side. Queen opens her eyes as Nathan runs a hand along the gentle slope of her spine. 'Queen will keep Nero in line.'

He continues stroking Queen, who begins to purr. It is an odd sound, like the distant hum of a swarm of wasps. Nan sees the affection in Nathan's caress, and feels a pang of jealousy. She averts her eyes as if she should not be a party to their intimacy. Nathan seems to sense her unease. He stops stroking Queen and moves a few inches away from her. Queen begins to clean herself where Nathan has been stroking.

'The man I saw you with,' he says. 'In the New Cut. Who was he?'

His bluntness startles her. A dozen answers fly through her head. 'My husband,' she says finally. She looks away, unable to meet his gaze when she is lying. 'We had a son,' she adds. 'A baby boy . . .' Her voice tails off. She does not know why she has mentioned the child.

'What happened?'

'He was weak . . . and lived for only eight weeks.'

'I'm sorry.' Nathan hesitates a moment. 'And your husband?'

'I left him. He went away to sea.'

'You danced with him that night.'

Nan hesitates, grateful that he does not know what else occurred. 'I hadn't seen him in a long time,' she explains. They sit in silence.

'He was here tonight. In the audience.'

Nan looks up sharply. 'You saw him?'

Nathan nods.

'He is jealous,' she murmurs. 'Though he has no reason to be,' she adds quickly. She looks again at Nathan, but his face is a mask.

'Then he is like Nero,' says Nathan.

And I am like Queen, she thinks with dismay. 'I'm very tired,' she says, for she cannot fight it any longer.

He goes to the door, drawing back the bolt, and Nan follows him out of the cage. 'You can stay here if you like,' he says, nodding in the direction of the bedroll.

Nan hesitates, unsure of his intentions. 'What of you?' she asks cautiously.

'I have a room nearby,' he says.

'Oh.' She cannot conceal the trace of disappointment in her voice.

Nathan misinterprets her response. 'Don't worry, you'll be safe here,' he says reassuringly. He takes a step closer, and for a moment Nan thinks that he will take her in his arms. 'Queen and Nero will watch over you,' he adds. They stare at each other, and Nan feels a sudden rush of longing. Nathan turns away.

She watches as he picks up a copper bucket by the stove. He opens the door and dumps a fresh load of coal inside. When he is finished, there is an awkward silence.

'I'll see you tomorrow,' he says, disappearing.

Nan stares at the bedroll. The boy seemed almost frightened of her, she thinks sadly. She should not have told him of her child.

30

Nathan

NATHAN RISES EARLY the next morning and hurries to the menagerie, but Nan is already gone. He stares down at the neatly folded bedroll with dismay. He had thought that she would wait for him, though he realises now she had no reason to.

He has slept badly. Their conversation has depressed him. He has spent the night brooding on the fact of her marriage and the child, for he trusts marriage and believes in its sanctity. He came of age amidst the casual couplings of the circus, and has always longed for something more. And though it is clear that Nan does not love her husband, she is still not free. The sailor is lurking in the corners of her life.

Nathan turns away from the bedroll. He does not know why the orange girl has lodged so deeply in his mind. He wanted to take her in his arms last night, but he didn't dare. He needs something, or someone, to tether him to his life, or he risks disappearing altogether. That is why he came to find his mother.

Queen breathes heavily in her sleep, like a horse. Her time is near. Nathan may be a man but even he can tell this, for she has begun almost to roll as she walks, and her manner is distracted. On his mother's instructions he has moved a large wooden box into the cage and filled it with clean straw. So far neither of the lions has touched it. Nero seems to know it's not for him, and cuts a wide berth around it when he paces the cage. Queen occasionally turns her gaze to it, as if to reassure herself that it is there.

Nathan goes behind the bar to dress his arm. He unwinds the strip of linen and carefully pours spirits along the length of the tear. The wound is a little inflamed around the edges, but it has nearly closed, and he suspects that his mother's warnings were inflated. He puzzles over her anger and, for the hundredth time, wonders whether she hasn't known it was him from the moment he arrived. That she would practise such deceit confounds him, for he can think of no earthly reason why; but he has never understood his mother. It would be folly to try now.

31

Nathan

THE DAY HIS mother leaves, Nathan is folded into Carla's family without a word. At night he shares a separate wagon with her children. For the first time he has brothers, sisters, even a father, Manny, who forces a smile whenever he is near. There are six children in all. The eldest, Lucia, is twelve. She will have little to do with the rest of them, unless she is put in charge. Next are the twins, a boy and girl of eight, who rarely leave each other's side. Nathan longs to slip between their locked elbows and be privy to their whispered secrets. Two more boys of six and five follow. They wrestle with each other constantly but turn on him like wild dogs whenever he tries to join in. Finally there is a girl of three, who wails loudly whenever he comes near.

The five eldest and Nathan sleep tightly packed as herrings in the wagon, while the youngest shares an adjoining wagon with her parents. On his first night, Carla defies their angry glares and clears a space for him at one end, where Nathan presses up against the canvas and shuts his eyes in the hope that he will simply disappear. The weeks pass and a grudging acceptance settles on the others like a layer of fine dust, but even after two months Nathan still does not feel one of them. His face is pointed and theirs are round, and when they speak they use the other language, the one he does not understand. Often they quarrel with one another, but they are careful not to fight with him, since it will draw the wrath of their mother. Sometimes he wishes she would not defend him, for with her stern looks and angry hisses, she drives them all away.

On his fourth birthday, there is a cake. It is small and round and iced in white, and decorated with the sugared peel of oranges. He is silent as Carla places it in front of him. Someone has made a coloured garland of paper flowers that they have draped about the plate, and next to it there is a small brown parcel tied with string. The other children lurk at a distance, waiting for a slice of cake, while the adults of the troupe gather round a little too closely. There is an awkward silence, and Nathan panics. He has no memory of an occasion such as this, and does not know what is expected of him. He can sense that they have laboured to make the day a special one, and it *is* memorable. Indeed, he will never forget it: this first birthday without her.

He stays with them for five years. When he is eight, Carla's husband, Manny, is injured during a riding accident. Manny is laid up for some weeks, and when he finally rises from his bed, his days as a performer are over. His left arm dangles

uselessly and he lopes rather than walks. The troupe rear-
ranges itself, just as it did when Nathan's mother disappeared, but Nathan feels the strain of his presence upon
Carla. One night at sunset he wanders over to Riza's wagon
and asks if he can stay. The strongman looks at him in surprise
and then, without a word, clears a space on the floor. That
first night Nathan lies awake for hours in the darkness of
Riza's wagon, while the strongman sits outside smoking by
his fire. The smell of woodsmoke and tobacco and the sweat
of Riza's things is like an enchantment that eventually lulls
him to sleep. When he wakes in the dead of night, he is
reassured by Riza's hulking presence at his side.

He is careful not to intrude upon the strongman's life. For
as long as he can remember, Riza has lived alone. By day
Nathan makes himself scarce, disappearing on his own, or
sometimes accompanied by Carla's two younger boys, who
are now his friends. He continues to take his meals with the
others, but at night he slips quietly back to Riza's wagon,
where the strongman has fashioned a sort of mattress upon
the floor out of the fragrant boughs of evergreens. In the
evenings they sit together by the fire, and Riza tells him
stories of the places they have been, places Nathan scarcely
remembers. At other times, they sprawl across the long grass
in silence, and Nathan throws his head back to the stars.

They share the wagon happily for many months, and for
the first time in his memory, Nathan is content. At the start
of the season, the troupe takes on some new members. Riza,
whose behaviour towards Nathan has always been calm and
consistent, becomes increasingly agitated. He spends hours
splitting logs behind the wagon, grunting with each blow, and

in the evenings he is prone to dark moods, which fall across him like a shadow. The changes puzzle Nathan, and he takes extra care in Riza's presence, the way he did around his mother. Then, one warm spring day, he returns unexpectedly to the wagon to retrieve his penknife. He hoists himself on to the flatbed, where in front of him Riza lies entwined around the limbs of a wiry French acrobat. Nathan sees the taut muscles of Giselle's back beneath the span of Riza's hands, can just make out her small breasts squashed flat against his chest. Giselle does not see him, but Riza does, and the fierce explosion in his eyes is enough to send Nathan reeling back upon the grass. He lands badly on one ankle, the pain shooting up his shin, and limps quickly away, his face burning.

That night he returns to Carla's wagon, and despite a round of protests from the others, squeezes in beside them. They have all sprouted inches in the intervening months, and the wagon is so full that Nathan can scarcely roll over in the darkness. The following morning he cannot meet Riza's eye, though later in the day the strongman lays a hand upon his shoulder and gives it a reassuring squeeze. Giselle moves her things into Riza's wagon, and within a few days the strongman begins to repair an old flatbed wagon for Nathan to occupy on his own. Nathan watches anxiously as Riza builds a frame out of willow saplings and covers it with strong canvas, then gathers timber for a simple wooden bunk. He even makes a small table and chair for Nathan's use, and after three days of hammering, the wagon is nearly ready. Riza appears the next morning, his muscled arms laden with tins of old scenery paint, and grins at Nathan. They work together. Nathan chooses blue for the floor, yellow for the walls, and green for the furniture, while Riza paints the outside of the wagon red.

Giselle visits from time to time, bringing jugs of sarsaparilla and salted nuts. She is small, with muscled shoulders and a narrow waist, and calves the size of grapefruits. Her long dark hair is pulled tightly from her face, and it swings like the tail of a horse when she walks. Her eyes are large and brown, and her nose a little too sharp, but there is a definite allure about her that even Nathan is aware of. She walks purposefully, with her toes pointed outward, even when she is not performing. And when she eats, she takes small, precise bites, chewing carefully, her perfect ivory teeth slightly bared. Nathan cannot help but watch. In her act she spins from a rope held in her mouth, and he wonders if her teeth are somehow different from his own. His can see the others watching her as well, and in this way Giselle reminds him of his mother. She is a little like a cat, he decides, deft and fluid in her movements, and distant in her manner. When she hoists herself up into the air, the sight of the small tuft of dark hair underneath each arm sends a jolt through him.

While Nathan and Riza paint, she sometimes lingers for a time, sitting on the edge of the flatbed and swinging her muscled calves in the air. She does not know how to speak to Nathan, and never meets his eye. Instead she flirts with Riza, who seems to swell like a sponge in her presence. Riza banters with her, and Nathan feels self-conscious, as if he is intruding on their courtship. After she goes, he is always relieved. He and Riza resume their work in silence. When the job is finished, Nathan is slightly alarmed by the result, for the wagon resembles a garish carousel; but it is not just the colours that unsettle him. Nathan looks at the wagon and understands that he is grown.

Riza helps him move his things into the wagon, and Carla presents him with a patchwork quilt she and Lucia have hastily pierced together from old remnants of clothes. Nathan is touched by the gift, as if she has surrendered some part of her family to him for ever. He sees at once in the quilt the chequered history of her children. That night, when he crawls beneath it, he shuts his eyes and imagines they still inhabit the small squares of fabric, their warm breath upon his face, their sprawling torsos shifting ceaselessly around him. The thought comforts him, and sleep comes more easily than he anticipated.

To his relief, Nathan discovers that the wagon does not maroon him as he feared. Indeed it has the opposite effect, for it enhances his status with the others. The twins, now fifteen, adopt him as a sort of mascot. They take to playing cards upon his bunk in the evenings, while the two younger boys moon about outside, longing to join in. After a few weeks, the painted floorboards of the wagon are covered with the muddy footprints of them all, and Nathan feels a sense of calm return. At night he sometimes hears Giselle's laughter reach across the darkness from their campfire.

He is given a horse and begins to accompany Manny on the long rides to scout sites and help with advance billing. He can see that Manny's health is deteriorating, that soon he will not be capable of such tasks. He does not know that he is being groomed for this role, part of the plan they have conceived on his behalf: Carla and Manny and Riza and the others. Giselle remains with the strongman for two seasons, though even Nathan can see her falling away. Towards the end she rarely smiles, and instead of laughter he hears their muffled arguments in the night. When she finally runs off with a young ranch-hand, Nathan feels the weight of their union rise up and fly away. Even Riza seems relieved. Gradually, the two resume their evenings by the fire. The strongman seems older to Nathan, and a little weary. His humour has a darker edge. But once again, he is Nathan's.

32

The Lions

QUEEN PACES BACK and forth inside the cage. Something is happening within her belly. She can feel the almost rhythmic tightening of her muscles, and knows that she must soon seek refuge in the box. She needs to escape the light and the prying eyes of those around her. She has avoided the box until now, for she was not quite ready to admit its purpose, but as she ducks inside for the first time and sinks down into the clean straw, she is grateful for its shelter. She nestles lower presenting the long curve of her spine to Nero and the world outside the cage. Although she is in pain, she feels relief that the moment is finally upon her, for she has spent too long in readiness. More and more she has lost the habit of anticipation. On the veldt, she sometimes sat for hours waiting for a kill, but her ability to do so has slowly ebbed. Now waiting only irritates her.

Nero, sensing her unease, has remained quietly in a corner since early this morning. He wishes he could ignore what is happening to Queen. It is completely separate from him, and he is powerless to stop it. Part of him longs to be the one inside the box, simply to escape the tedium of life within the cage.

Nero sees her long tongue panting and the glassiness in her eyes, and knows that he should not disturb her. Instead he squeezes himself into the corner of the cage and rests his head upon his paws. He thinks a little irritably of the boy and the meat that he will bring, for his mind always runs to food when he is bored. He will have to wait: wait for food, wait for Queen, wait for the moment when the world inside the cage is right again. He does not know how long.

He listens to Queen pant, to the struggling of her body against the sides of the box and the almost continuous rustling of the straw. Queen gives a loud moan: a long, low, plaintive groan that he has never heard before. The sound makes his fur rise. He raises his head to search for the boy, but does not find him. Kezia's face appears briefly on the other side of the tent, staring out at him. She too has heard Queen, and has emerged from her box to investigate, before concealing herself again in the straw. Nero is pleased to see her, for he does not want to be alone with Queen and her strange noises. But where is the cage boy? Nero wishes he were here.

33

Nathan

SOME HOURS LATER Nathan stands on his favourite spot on London Bridge. For once the fog has lifted and the winter sun is almost warm upon his back. He leans right out over the parapet, tracing the constant flow of traffic beneath him, and momentarily forgets himself. That is his objective. He does not wish to think of Nan or Nero or his mother, nor of the bungled purpose of his journey. He feels at home on the parapet, and has stayed much longer than he intended. Nathan does this without realising: colonises a particular place, returns to it again and again until it becomes a part of him.

He is startled by a church bell ringing in the distance. He does not wish to be reminded of the time. The bridge is crowded, and someone jostles him from behind. People push through the traffic as if their very lives depend on their ability to reach the other side. Only Nathan remains still. He knows he must present a strange sight, but doesn't care.

After a moment he feels someone at his elbow, and turns

to see an odd-looking man stop beside him. It is rare that Nathan speaks to strangers in this city, rarer still for him to be approached, and he is immediately on his guard. But he is also disconcerted, for there is something in the stranger's manner that mirrors his own, as if they are both equally out of place and time. The man is small in build like himself but some years older, and his clothes are well-made but threadbare. He is dressed entirely in black, lending him the look of a clergyman, though his clothes are far too foppish for the church, and the look in his eyes is one of anticipation. He wears a smart-looking black silk hat, the sort that gentlemen wear in the evening, and now he removes it and bows deferentially to Nathan. Nathan feels himself recoil.

The man does not appear to notice. He balances the hat on his palm, and with a neat flick of his wrist sends it spinning into the air above his head. The hat lands neatly in the crook of his outstretched arm, and with a snap of his elbow the man sends it flying up into the air again. The hat spins several times and this time lands upside down upon his head. The man tilts his head backwards, sending the hat tumbling down behind him, where it lands on his foot. With a kick he sends the hat airborne once again, and then volleys it back and forth between his head, shoulders and upturned elbows.

Nathan watches the display wide-eyed. He does not know its purpose, nor why the man has singled him out for his attentions. He is conscious that a few passers-by have paused to watch, and feels his face reddening. The man continues to fling the hat higher and higher, never once using his hands, and Nathan can hear only the soft thud of silk against his skin. Then the man tosses the hat nearly twice as high as before, and Nathan watches as it spins downwards from the sky and lands squarely on his head. The man smiles, a broad, knowing grin that Nathan instantly recognises, and extends both hands out in front of him.

An entertainer! Thinks Nathan with alarm. The fact embarrasses him, not only because he did not recognise it earlier, but because there is something untoward about one entertainer performing for another. Nathan feels almost certain that had the man known his trade, he would not have approached him. However, there is nothing about Nathan's person to suggest that he is one of them: he is unrecognisable even to his own kind, and this unsettles him. He stares at the man, wanting somehow to communicate the fact of their brotherhood, but finds himself unable. The hat-man's smile disappears, and Nathan sees a flash of anger in his eyes, no doubt because he thinks he will not be rewarded for his efforts. Nathan reaches somewhat belatedly into his pockets and his fingers clutch at the empty fabric. The hat-man eyes him icily for a moment, then turns expectantly towards the small crowd that has gathered to watch. They disperse instantly, striding away with their eyes averted, leaving the hat-man empty-handed. He turns to Nathan one last time, and the look in his eyes is one of outright hostility. Then he turns on his heels and disappears into the crowd.

Nathan stands motionless in the hat-man's wake. He feels bruised by the man's anger, and suddenly weary. He thinks of a summer's night on the prairie: a night so hot and windless that he and Riza are forced to bed down in the open grass to avoid the stifling heat of the wagons. But it is too hot for sleep, and Nathan stares up at the stars. Riza rolls over and sighs, and Nathan realises that he too is awake. The strong-man sits up and fishes in his pockets for a smoke. Nathan sees the match flare, and the strong smell of tobacco envelops him. He sits up. Riza's enormous bulk seems to have diminished in the darkness, and for the first time Nathan sees him as he is: nothing but an ordinary man.

Riza catches his stare and smiles, and Nathan looks away, embarrassed. His eyes travel over the darkness: the wagons, the horses, the tall grass, which stretches as far as he can see.

'Sometimes I wish that we could stop,' he says.

Riza looks at him with mock severity. 'Stop what? Breathing?'

Nathan blushes, for Riza is not one to mince words, nor to allow others to mince them. 'Stop moving. Stop performing. Stop all of this.' Nathan sweeps an arm over the row of wagons.

'Why should we?'

Nathan shrugs. He does not know. 'To rest,' he says finally.

Riza considers this. 'But I am not tired,' he says. 'Why should I want to rest?' He takes a deep puff of his cigarette and carefully exhales the smoke in rings. Nathan watches as the neat smoke circles float off in the night, like a tiny aerial performance.

'Besides,' continues Riza, 'when you stop, the world outside does not shine so brightly. The lights are dim. And the applause is not so loud.' He looks at Nathan then and grins a little sheepishly.

Nathan smiles in return, but what he really thinks is that

applause is like a demon. He wonders fleetingly whether that is what happened to his mother: whether she was not carried away on the back of a devil in the dead of night.

'What were you before?' he asks.

Riza frowns. 'Before, I was weak. And unlucky.' He stares disdainfully at the half-smoked cigarette in his fingers, as if it is the stub of his old life.

'And what happened?'

'I became strong.'

'But what of your home?' says Nathan. 'And your people?'

Riza raises his arm to indicate the vast darkness around him. 'This is my home. These are my people.' Then, seeing Nathan's disbelief, he raises a finger and wags it forcefully. 'It is enough. It is as much as anyone has.'

Nathan stares at him. He has no way of knowing whether Riza speaks the truth. 'Sometimes I feel that we are trapped,' he says finally. 'Sometimes I feel that we are caged, like the animals in the menagerie, and that all the world has come to stare at us.'

Riza raises an eyebrow. 'Then it is a cage of our own making. We hold the key. We can leave at any time if we choose. We simply do not wish to. In a sense, we are more free than those outside. We have no rules, no boundaries, no ties, nothing that binds us to the ordinary world. That is our privilege and our blessing.'

Nathan frowns. He does not feel blessed. But he trusts Riza more than anyone alive, and wants with all his heart to live by his words, for he has no others to guide him. He lies back with a sigh, staring at the vast expanse of stars. 'When you are older, you will see,' says Riza, tossing the remains of his cigarette into the darkness. 'The world is not so forgiving as you think.' Riza eases himself down into his own bedroll. His voice floats up to Nathan out of the night. 'It is a savage place.'

34

The Lions

QUEEN PANTS AND pants. Her entire body feels buoyant, as if it is floating in the aftermath of birth. The pain is over but the shock of it stays with her; she shakes her head but cannot free herself from its grip. Beside her on the floor are the cubs: nothing more than tiny inert sacs of fur. There are two of them, and she knows instinctively that one is dead. The other lifts its tiny nose from time to time and quivers, but otherwise lies still, exhausted from the ordeal of its journey. The cubs are covered in blood and muck. She knows that she must clean them, but her own mouth is so dry that she does not yet feel able. She sees the water bowl on the far side of the cage and wills it to be nearer, for she does not trust her legs to carry her even the short distance to where it lies.

Beside her, the live cub begins to mewl pathetically. It raises its head in her direction, its blind eyes turned towards her face, sensing that she is there. She shrinks back and stares at it with detached interest. So this is what she has been waiting for, this tiny ball of fur, born in a wooden box of straw instead of in the long grasses of the veldt. The sight of its trembling body disturbs her, for she has learned to trust nothing since she came into the cage. Perhaps it isn't real. Perhaps it is a dream that she will soon wake from. But the tiny cub continues to mewl, directing its plaintive cries in her direction, until it finally collapses with exhaustion.

Queen is grateful for the silence that follows. She turns her gaze to the other cub. Something about its motionless form fills her with relief, for she does not understand how she is supposed to bring a cub into the world of men – a world of sawdust and flickering light, butchered meat and cracking whips. Nothing in her experience has prepared her for the prospect.

She feels hot and irritated, and the thirst rages in her throat. With an enormous effort she heaves herself to her feet and walks the few steps to the bowl of water laid out for her. Her legs tremble as she walks, and she can feel the loose folds of her abdomen sway beneath her. The feeling disconcerts her, for she has grown used to the tautness in her belly these past few weeks. When she reaches the water, she feels suddenly nauseous, and turns aside to retch. For the second time that day, she cannot control her body.

When she has finished retching, she sinks down on to her haunches. The taste of bile is in her mouth. She musters her energy and leans forward, turning her head sideways so as to drink deeply. She closes her eyes and as she drinks, she has the sudden image that she is swimming in the middle of a river. The swift current rushes past her, and she feels her body being carried along by its force, until she is finally pulled under. The current drags her deep below the water's surface, and she is surprised by how cool and clean the water feels on her face. She surrenders herself to it, floats freely on the rushing tide, until the persistent crying of the cub finally raises her, unwilling, to the surface.

35

Nathan

I T IS EARLY afternoon when Nathan finally returns to the menagerie. Talliot and his mother are waiting for him. He sees that Queen's time has come, for in his absence they have transferred Nero to another, smaller cage, and have covered Queen's cage with huge sheets of sailcloth so she may have seclusion. He feels dismay that he was not here, and anger that his mother should have been the one to discover her. He wonders how she knew. Was it simply female intuition? Why did he not realise when he saw Queen heave her swollen girth across the cage at dawn this morning?

He hears a muffled feline moan through the canvas. The sound is unlike any he has ever heard, but before he can conceal his alarm, he knows his mother has seen it. Nathan asks what else can be done.

'There is nothing more,' says his mother, with the authority of her sex. 'We must leave her now. It is her first litter and she will need some time to adjust. We will close the menagerie for the evening. Keep the tent warm, and make sure that she has plenty of water. But do not disturb her in any way.'

Nathan nods. 'And the act?' he asks, hoping she will cancel it.

His mother turns to Nero and frowns. 'Nero will have to perform alone. He has always lived in Queen's shadow, but now he must become a star in his own right.'

She orders Talliot to wheel Nero's cage into the main tent, and when he is gone she faces Nathan. 'You will have to work him twice as hard. The act must be a constant challenge for him. You must make him forget that he is on his own. There must be no break in the routine, and the timing must be accurate to the second. Do you understand?'

Nathan nods dumbly. He feels a sudden bond with Nero, for they are both at her mercy.

'All will be well,' she says, reading his doubts. She pauses, measuring his worth.

'You were born to work with them,' she says. 'Just as my husband was. We were very fortunate to find you.' She begins slowly to wheel herself across the tent towards the door. Nathan feels her sliding away from him once again. He knows that he must stop her.

'It wasn't luck that brought me here,' he calls out suddenly. His mother stops, but does not turn to face him. In the silence that follows, Nathan hears Queen rustle in her straw. 'I've been looking for you,' he says. 'I've been looking for you all my life.'

His mother slowly turns her chair round to face him. Her body is completely still. 'I do not know what you mean,' she says, pronouncing each word distinctly.

He stares at her, unsure how to proceed. 'You toured with

the mud circus in America,' he says finally. His voice sounds small and remote.

Her eyes narrow before she replies. 'I performed in many places.'

Nathan takes a deep breath. 'There was a child,' he says. 'You had a son.'

His mother looks at him. 'Yes,' she says evenly.

'It was me.'

His mother frowns. 'Someone has played a cruel joke on you,' she says. Her face is like granite, but he can hear a fault line in her voice. 'My son is dead.'

Nathan blinks, for he does not know what to make of her words.

'He was born weak and died very young. It was a blessing,' she continues, 'an act of mercy, for he would never have survived.'

Nathan catches his breath. 'But I remember you,' he says.

'Perhaps you do. Perhaps, like many others, you saw me perform. Perhaps you even knew me as a child. But you are not my son.' Her voice is flat, her tone final.

Nathan stares at her. He cannot trust his child's memory, for it is possible that she is right. Perhaps the woman he remembers is a trick of his imagination: a desperate effort to save himself. An act of mercy. She turns her chair again as if to go.

'The boy who died,' he says impulsively. 'What was his name?'

'He was named for his father,' she says slowly. 'My husband.'

Mad Jack, thinks Nathan. The Lion King. His mind is

spinning now. 'And did you think of him?' he says urgently. 'Your son? Did you think of him afterwards?'

She looks at him intently and Nathan feels that she may bury him under the weight of her gaze. 'What kind of mother would I be if I did not?'

Nathan stares down at the sawdust on the floor, for he can no longer meet her eyes. The blood rushes in his ears and mingles with the sound of wheels rolling in the dust. When he finally raises his head to find his mother, she is gone.

36

Nan

FOR THE DURATION of the strikes, Nan and Shad hide away. The rookery is a world where they can easily lose themselves. Shad returns every now and then with a handful of coins. She does not ask where they come from. And though she would not admit it, Nan needs to be lost. She has been stunned by this new self, the one she has given bodily to Shad. She did not know it existed.

But Shad is not surprised. It is as if he caught a glimpse inside her years before. When Shad lays her down at night and runs his hands between her legs, Nan is both enthralled and ashamed. In the morning, she shuts her eyes and tries to forget what is happening.

More and more, she retreats into the past. One night when she is lying in his arms, she is overtaken by a memory. Shad is very young, perhaps four or five, and they have left him in her charge. She has dragged him down to the river at low tide, for she likes the feel of mud between her toes, and has inherited her father's taste for scavenging. They scamper about for a time, finding nothing more than a lead pipe and an old rope, when she sees the glint of metal near the water's edge. She races to the spot and roots out a small bronze coin. She sees at once that it is very old, recognises the hammered edge and battered Roman stamp upon its face. Shad appears by her side.

'Treasure,' she tells him with a grin. He stares at the coin. 'Help me dig,' she orders, kneeling down in the mud. 'If we find more, we'll be rich.' She begins to dig with her hands. Shad watches for a moment, then joins her enthusiastically. They scoop up hand after hand of mud in their fingers, but find nothing. After several minutes Nan sits back on her haunches with a sigh. She sees that the tide has turned and is slowly crawling towards them.

'C'mon, Shad,' she says, standing up. He squints up at her against the late afternoon sun.

'What about the others?'

'There are no others.'

Shad blinks a few times, taking in this information, then slowly stands, wiping his muddy hands on his trousers.

'Come on. The tide is rising. We have to go.'

'Where?' He looks at her, confused.

'Home,' she says, exasperated.

'But you said we'd be rich.'

She sighs and grabs his hand, pulling him away from the lapping water.

'Not today.'

'When?' He is staring at her hand, the one holding the coin. She takes his palm and puts the coin in it, wrapping his tiny fingers tightly round.

'Maybe never.'

They return home, and that evening, she sees him show the coin to Auntie. 'Mam, are we rich?' he asks.

Auntie peers at the coin with mild interest. 'Not hardly,' she says. 'But you could buy your mam a drink if you wanted.' She throws back her head and laughs, does not see Shad glower across the room at Nan. After they're in bed, tucked up in opposite ends of the same mattress, his voice floats up to her.

'You're a liar.'

'It was only pretend, Shad. Make-believe.'

Shad wrestles with her words for a moment.

'There's no such thing,' he says stubbornly.

Lying in his arms in the rookery, Nan is beginning to understand that Shad can still not separate what is real from what is not. It is as if he does not know how to fold himself into the world. He is the wrong shape somehow, or perhaps the wrong size, or constructed of the wrong material. What Shad needs is his own world. One that runs parallel to the other, like the lines of a railway. And he needs her.

She eases herself up on one elbow, and stares down at his sleeping figure. She is not sure that she can spend her life in Shad's small universe. She is not certain that she should be there even now. She falls asleep wondering what will happen if she leaves him.

When she wakes in the morning, the stone of sickness is inside her. She creeps into the hallway, where she retches into a bucket. When the sickness subsides, she lies back down upon the bed, careful not to wake Shad. She closes her eyes and a picture slowly forms in her mind: Shad's mother sweating in the doorway, her trembling hands splayed about her rock-hard belly. Nan knows then that she is carrying his child.

She does not tell him for some weeks, until she has had a chance to absorb the fact of it herself. When she finally confronts him with the truth, he looks at her uncomprehending.

'A child,' she repeats. 'Yours and mine.'

Shad's face fills with alarm. 'Can you stop it?' he asks cautiously.

She lays a hand upon her belly. 'No,' she says decisively, for she can still deceive him, just as she did when they were young. Shad looks down at her belly as if it is a stranger who has suddenly appeared at the door.

'Then we have no choice,' he says slowly.

'No.'

'We will have to let it come.'

'Yes.'

But Shad does not want to let it come. Nan quickly sees this. He refuses to speak of what is happening in her body, and does not touch her in the same way. At night, he reaches for her only from behind, and when she turns herself to face him, he shuts his eyes. By day, he disappears for long periods of time, returning with the dirt of the city soaked into his skin. Eventually, when she is heavily pregnant, he takes to drinking like his mam, though this at least he tries to conceal from her. As the weeks pass, Nan feels as if they are swimming back in time, that she and Shad are somehow trapped inside their mothers' lives. But as the birth nears, her fears begin to ebb. She turns inward. She cannot think of Shad, or his mam, or her own. She can think only of the tiny child, bobbing deep inside her.

37

Nathan

NATHAN IS IN the ring again. The whip feels like a bludgeon in his hand and Nero appears twice his normal size, but otherwise he feels fine. He has been drinking steadily and with quiet determination for the past six hours, ever since his mother, or the woman who claims she is not his mother, wheeled herself away from him. He has finished the remains of a large bottle of apple brandy he pilfered from behind the bar, together with nearly half a bottle of something else he failed to identify, whose flavour reminded him of sassafras tea. He is not normally a drinker: the effect of both drinks on his system has been both instantaneous and wide-ranging. He is not quite seeing double at the moment but, when he squints, Nero appears to wear a golden ray of light around his mane, like a halo. The effect is almost biblical, and Nathan wonders briefly whether he should introduce a lamb to his act, now that Queen is unable to perform.

He has been drunk on only one other occasion. The night

before his eighteenth birthday, Riza pitched up outside his wagon with a jug of moonshine in his hand. They drank and smoked until dawn, the strongman throwing back three tumblers to his one, with the result that when the sun finally rose Nathan was slumped unconscious in the grass. Riza never slurred a word. Nathan awoke only when Riza heaved him on to his bunk. He spent the next twenty-four hours vomiting, and in his darkest hour Nathan swore never to drink again in this lifetime.

But now he is dead, according to his mother, so he felt entitled to indulge himself behind the bar this afternoon. The result is that he is now standing in the ring with Nero patiently awaiting a signal he cannot remember. He hears a catcall from the audience, and in response cracks the whip loudly in the air. Nero gives a start and even Nathan finds the noise deafening, but the audience stirs excitedly and he hears a smattering of applause. Emboldened, Nathan begins to stumble through his act. To his surprise, far from being edgy without Queen, Nero is alarmingly well-mannered and compliant.

Nathan rather likes the feel of the whip in his hand and cracks it needlessly every few moments. He succeeds in rousing the crowd but Nero becomes increasingly agitated, and snarls nervously each time he brings the whip down. Nathan ignores the obvious signs of his confusion. He arranges a series of pedestals in a circle around the outside of the ring in preparation for Nero's final stunt: a trick they have practised only twice before. Nathan gives the signal and Nero leaps deftly from one to the next, gathering speed until he appears to be flying about the ring in leaps and bounds.

The crowd erupts with approval, and Nathan urges Nero to quicken his pace, until the fur about his shoulders begins to darken with sweat and specks of foam appear at the corners of his jaw. Nathan cracks the whip again and again, taunting Nero, until suddenly the lion stumbles and misses his footing. His enormous bulk collides with a pedestal, sending it flying across the ring. Nero tumbles sideways to the floor in a blurry somersault of fur, accompanied by a screeching yowl. In the next instant, he rights himself and turns angrily on Nathan, crouching low and flattening his ears, ready to spring.

Nathan stops short, his chest heaving, the flare of the gas lamps suddenly painfully bright. Nero's eyes glow green with rage, sending an icy shot of fear right through Nathan's veins. He has never seen Nero in such a state and feels suddenly unequal to the task. He must pacify the lion and remove him from the ring at once.

He reaches in the tiny leather pouch where he keeps a few choice morsels of horseflesh, and throws the entire contents in Nero's direction. The meat lands at Nero's feet and for a split second Nero looks as if he would prefer Nathan, before leaping upon the meat instead, lapping it up with his enormous tongue. Nathan waits for him to finish, then cautiously signals for Nero to leave the cage, never once glancing up at the audience. The crowd reacts badly: they know that Nathan has curtailed the act. They whistle and bay and call for more. And when he leaves the ring behind him, he hears a collective groan of disappointment.

38

The Lions

QUEEN LONGS FOR escape. They have darkened the cage, but now its walls are closing in on her. The cloth is dank and heavy, and the smell of mildew burns her nostrils. For once she craves the sight of iron bars and human faces, the world beyond the cloth, if only for a moment. Somewhere outside, the crowd gives a sudden roar of excitement. It is showtime, and Queen paces back and forth restlessly, images of Nathan and Nero and the painted wooden pedestals flashing in her brain. She hears the whip again and again, and the harsh crack of it excites her, makes her long for the high-pitched frenzy of the ring.

Her body still feels sore from the birth. She is anxious to recover her former self: to stretch and spring and sprint, and feel the taut clench of muscled flesh between her jaws. This is what she desires most: a chance to lose herself once more in the long grass and shimmering heat of the veldt. A chance to run as fast as her bruised and aching bones will take her, to run without stopping until she has passed over the horizon.

Behind her, inside the now-soiled wooden box, the tiny spotted cub whines and whines. Its eyes are open but the cub grows weaker by the hour, for Queen has refused to suckle it since it was born. Indeed, she has not looked inside the box in several hours, preferring to put as much distance as she can between herself and the wrinkled mound of skin and bones, which now cries almost ceaselessly. The noise is like the constant hum of the cicada: it disconcerted her at first but now she does not hear it. And the excited sounds from the crowd have made her temporarily forget the box and its contents. In the far corner of the cage, underneath a pile of straw, lies the inert body of the other cub. Queen glances at it from time to time as she paces, and the sight of it snags something inside her.

She hears the crowd hoot and whistle, and wonders what has brought on their response. And then she hears Nero yowl: a jarring scream which sets her fur on edge. The crowd erupts in response, shouting and stamping their feet. Queen freezes, straining to hear Nero. The crowd dies down. For a long, curious moment there is silence. She listens intently but can hear nothing from the ring.

Suddenly the mewling starts again from inside the cage: this time louder and more insistent. She turns her head towards the wooden box and sees the cub teetering on the edge, struggling to locate her in the gloom of the shrouded cage. Queen stares at the cub: at its tiny, shivering form and pathetic, half-blind gaze, and feels suddenly dizzy. The cub takes an uncertain step forward and topples head first from the wooden box on to the ground, landing in a crumpled heap. Once again it doggedly raises itself up and tries to take another step, only to fall again. It continues to whine, the pitch of its cry becoming hysterical. Queen watches as the cub, sensing her presence, drags itself across the floor of the cage towards the place where she remains frozen in the half-darkness. It finally collapses only a few feet from where she stands.

Queen stares down at the cub. Outside the crowd shouts again, but this time it is not excitement she can hear, but anger. They jeer and whistle and the sound echoes deep inside her. The tiny cub is silent now, its chest heaving from the effort of the journey, its head bobbing up and down. Queen can smell its scent: the sweet, slightly sickening smell of blood and mucus. The cub begins to move once more, inching its way towards her in a final, desperate effort. Queen struggles to focus her gaze upon the cub but her mind overflows with images: the crowded sea of faces in the ring, the dark flash of Nathan's whip, the jagged strike of lightning on the veldt, the soft throat of an impala. The pictures blind her for the moment, and the crowd's roar is deafening. She sees a flash of white before her eyes and lunges at it, feeling the tiny snap of bones between her jaws.

39

Nan

NAN WATCHES IN the wings as Nathan lurches through his act. The sight is almost more than she can bear. It dredges up that other time, when as a child she used to watch her mother stumble in the street and pitch forward. More than once, her mother fell so hard she did not rise. Each time, Nan would plant herself resolutely on the pavement by her side. Now what she remembers most about her mother is her smell. She chewed the rind of orange to mask the odour of gin upon her breath, and while Nan cannot tolerate the smell of gin, the scent of oranges will never leave her.

She watches in horror as Nero stumbles and spins on Nathan. She feels her insides plunge. Nathan's face is pinched and white in the harsh flare of the gas lamps, and the look in his eyes is one of dread. As he finishes the act and coaxes Nero out of the ring, the mood of the crowd turns sour. Nan stares at the crowd uncomprehendingly. What is it they desire, she wonders. Is it blood? Would they have man or beast emerge triumphant from the ring?

As Nathan finishes the act and makes his exit, a small crowd surges forward to buy oranges. Nan is repelled by the flushed excitement in their faces. She longs to turn her back on them and run. One by one she takes their pennies and offers her fruit until there is only one child remaining, a well-dressed lad of eight or nine. His cheeks are pink with excitement, but what strikes Nan most about him is his apparent innocence, as if the sullied waters of the crowd have somehow parted to allow him through. The boy holds his penny out expectantly and Nan freezes. Her mind conjures all of them at once: her wee boy, Shad, and Nathan as he must have been. The boy waits anxiously for her to take his penny. He shuffles from foot to foot, glances over his shoulder to where his parents must be seated in the crowd, then turns back to her with pleading eyes. When at last she takes his coin, he scuttles away from her, clutching his oranges to his chest like a thief.

40
Nathan

NATHAN SITS ALONE in the dark outside the menagerie. He wishes he were sober. He would like to rise and walk but his feet and legs seem somehow disconnected from his brain. He lies back upon the cold, damp earth and shuts his eyes. For the first time he feels desperately homesick. He yearns for land and space and the unbroken line of the horizon. He even misses his people: their loud voices and too-familiar ways. In his mind he suddenly takes flight, leaves his body lying motionless upon the ground, and takes to the sky. Like an albatross, he wheels across the dark waters of the Atlantic, and comes to rest once again in the long grasses of the prairie.

He must not think of his mother. When he came out of the ring this evening he caught a glimpse of her waiting in the wings, her arms rigid against the sides of the wheelchair, her face mottled with disgust. It's always the booze that wrecks a tamer. It is true that he feels wrecked, though he does not blame the drink. He wonders why her husband lost his nerve, and whether she had a hand in his undoing. He hears the crowd hoot with delight, knows that Lulu is airborne somewhere inside the tent. If only he could soar above the heads of those around him he might then gain the perspective that he needs.

The crowd erupts again with pleasure and Nathan presses his palms flat against the ground. He needs to halt the endless spinning in his head. He closes his eyes and concentrates on slowing down.

Some time later – he does not know how long – Nathan wakes and all is silent. The ground feels cold and hard against his back. He sits up, only to feel the dizzying rush of nausea return and looks around him in the darkness. He cannot have been asleep for long, for he can still feel the effects of brandy all too well. With relief he realises that the evening's performance is over and the crowds have all gone home. Somewhat unsteadily, he rises to his feet, and endeavours to brush the dirt from his coat. He hears a noise behind him in the darkness, and turns to see Lulu in a dark red gown, watching him with curiosity.

Nathan feels himself colour in the darkness.

'Are you all right?' Lulu asks.

Nathan nods. 'I guess I fell asleep,' he says.

Lulu looks around. 'There are better places,' he suggests with an arch of an eyebrow.

Nathan smiles a little. It is almost a relief to hear Lulu make fun of him and he takes some comfort in the thick curl of Lulu's accent. He forgets sometimes that they are both strangers here. He runs a hand through his hair.

'And now?' Lulu looks at him expectantly. Nathan shrugs a little nervously.

'You will return to your room?' ventures Lulu.

Nathan nods, thinks fleetingly of the bare room he rents, with its ochre-stained walls and grimy windowpane.

'Alone?'

Nathan looks at him. 'Yes.'

'You are tired?' Lulu asks.

Nathan hesitates, for the night air has suddenly cleared his head. 'No,' he answers.

'Then you should come with me,' says Lulu matter-of-factly.

'Where?'

'To a club I know. There will be music, champagne. The company of others. You will like it.'

Nathan looks at Lulu. The company of others. He has had precious little these past three months.

'All right,' he says, feeling somewhat reckless. Then he looks down at his clothes with dismay, for under his coat he is still dressed in circus costume: a tight tunic of suede with breeches to match. 'My clothes,' he ventures uncertainly.

Lulu shrugs. 'You're a lion tamer. What can people expect?'

❧

They walk out on to Westminster Bridge Road, where Lulu immediately hails a hansom. Nathan is not in the habit of taking cabs and he turns to Lulu uncertainly, for he has little money in his pockets. Lulu dismisses his concern with a wave of his hand. Nathan climbs inside the cab and as Lulu instructs the driver, his spirits suddenly lift. He leans back in the padded leather seat, glad for once to have a destination. The cab crosses over the river and carries on through the centre of the West End. It is Saturday night and the crowds are thick around the theatres of the Haymarket. The streets are filled with pedestrians and the cab must stop frequently in order to let them pass. Occasionally Nathan catches the eyes of those walking by, but mostly it is Lulu who draws attention in his low-cut crimson dress. Nathan sees the men look from Lulu to him and back again, and realises that they are envious. He shifts uncomfortably in his seat, and Lulu looks at him and smiles. 'You must relax,' he says, laying a gloved hand on Nathan's arm. Nathan can feel Lulu's warmth through the glove, but after a moment Lulu removes his hand and folds it neatly in his lap, the way a woman does.

The cab finally comes to a halt outside an imposing house somewhere behind Tottenham Court Road. Nathan waits as Lulu settles the fare.

'What is this place?' he asks.

'A club,' says Lulu. 'A private club. For very private people. One must be a member to enter, but you may come as my guest.' Lulu holds out his elbow, and Nathan sees he must take it. He glances up nervously at the house, wondering whether he has made a mistake to come. Heavy curtains are drawn across the windows, though he can see the welcoming glow of gaslight from within.

'If you do not like it, we will leave,' says Lulu then, seeing the doubt in Nathan's eyes. Nathan nods and takes Lulu's arm and together they climb the steps. Lulu pulls the bell and the door is opened by an elegantly dressed older woman in a dark green crinoline. Her silver hair is bound in wide circles round her head, and her face is heavily coated with powder, but Nathan still thinks she is attractive. The woman's face creases with pleasure when she sees Lulu.

'Darling, you're exquisite,' she says, leaning forward to give Lulu a hug. She turns to Nathan and extends a hand. 'And how good of you to bring a friend.'

'The boy must have champagne at once,' says Lulu jovially. 'And oysters. We are famished.'

'Yes, of course.'

The woman places a hand against the small of Nathan's back and ushers them inside, guiding them down some thickly carpeted stairs. Halfway down, they squeeze past a couple mounting slowly, a stout older man with an enormous moustache accompanied by a tall, thin brunette half his age. The man whispers something in the woman's ear as they pass and she throws back her head and gives a deep, velvety laugh. Nathan cannot help but glance back at them, for their pairing strikes him oddly. But as he does the man catches his eye and raises an eyebrow, and Nathan feels himself quickly colour.

They reach the bottom and enter an enormous room lit by dozens of candles. The walls are painted a deep orange and are hung with gilded mirrors all around, which catch the candlelight and throw it back upon the occupants. The room is crowded and Nathan glances quickly round. With relief he sees well-dressed men and women of all ages chatting amiably. Many are smoking and the air is heavy with haze. In the corner a trio of musicians accompanies a singer, an enormous woman with painted eyes and jet-black hair, who sways from side to side as she sings. Her voice is low and breathy, and Nathan can hardly make out the words over the sounds of those conversing around him. Lulu places a cold glass of champagne in his hand and orders him to drink. Nathan has never tasted champagne before and its fizzy sweetness startles him, but he enjoys the sensation and the cold drink slips easily down his throat.

'Come and sit,' says Lulu taking his arm again. They move through the crowd and find a small table near the singer. Across the room, a blonde woman with a double strand of pearls at her throat waves a hand in Lulu's direction. Nathan sees a brief flash of disdain on Lulu's face before he returns the wave. Lulu turns away and Nathan watches as the blonde woman leans over to whisper in the ear of her companion.

'Who is that woman?' asks Nathan.

'An acquaintance, nothing more,' says Lulu. 'She draws attention to herself by waving.'

Nathan frowns.

'You are new,' says Lulu with a smile. 'New faces are of interest. That is all.'

Nathan looks around him, disconcerted by the idea that once again he is an outsider. He shifts a little uncomfortably.

'Am I the only new face here?' he asks.

Lulu peruses the room for a moment, then shakes his head. 'There are others,' he says reassuringly. 'One at least,' he adds with a teasing glance.

Nathan drinks his champagne and feels the bubbles burst in his head. He turns to Lulu.

'Has Nan been here?'

Lulu looks at him and frowns. 'No,' he says. He starts to add something, then hesitates, chewing the corner of his mouth. Finally he takes a deep breath and speaks slowly, trapping Nathan's gaze steadily in his own. 'She would not be allowed, you see. Women are forbidden.'

Nathan looks at Lulu, but in his mind he sees the tall, thin woman on the stairs, hears her deep, velvety laugh, and sees the dark bulge at her throat as she throws back her head. He feels a fool.

'Forgive me,' says Lulu quietly. 'I thought you knew.' He looks away then, evidently embarrassed, and takes a small sip of his champagne. Nathan swallows and looks at the corpulent singer. For the first time he sees the dark shadow on her upper lip. He stares until the woman who greeted them at the door passes by with champagne. She pauses to fill both their glasses and Nathan cannot bring himself to meet her gaze. Instead he watches his glass, watches the bubbles travel quickly upwards in a steady stream, then gradually subside.

'But we should drink to her,' says Lulu suddenly. He holds up his glass and smiles brightly. Nathan hesitates a moment, then picks up his own.

'To Nan,' says Lulu, bringing the lip of his glass up to Nathan's.

Nathan nods, but cannot bring himself to echo the toast. He listens to the clink of the glasses, then brings his own to his lips and drinks deeply. His mind is swimming now. He cannot fight the lazy tug of current in his brain. It is the current that brought him here, he thinks. The current will have to carry him back home.

Many hours later Nathan wakes. Beside him Lulu sleeps on his stomach, his face turned towards him. Nathan can just make out the faint sound of his breath on the bedclothes. Nathan lies completely still, immobilised by the gathering storm in his mind. Cautiously, he allows his eyes to drift about the room. Through the cracks in the curtain he can see the faint winter sun, and from the street below he can hear the sounds of passers-by: a horse and carriage rattling along the cobblestones, a man's shouted curse and, somewhere off in the distance, a baby wailing. He gingerly raises himself up on one elbow. A jolt of pain runs through his head and he lies back down. He shuts his eyes and concentrates on the thumping ache in his brain and the sour taste in his mouth. He does not wish to think of what has happened.

He remembers dozing off in the hansom, the side of his head lolling on to the angled bone of Lulu's shoulder. He remembers the cab lurching to a stop: the jangling sound of the horse's bit against its teeth, the sullen indifference of the driver as he and Lulu stumbled out of the cab. He remembers dancing, both at the club and afterwards at the flat, where Lulu played the piano. He remembers the surprisingly solid warmth of Lulu in his arms, the taut feel of muscles along his back, and the slightly sweet, musky odour of his scent. He remembers falling over, upsetting his glass in the process, and the sudden pull of Lulu's arm as he was led along a darkened hall. Finally he remembers laughing, as one by one, Lulu grasped the heels of his boots and pulled with all his strength. The boots refused to budge at first, but then gave way all at once. Just as he himself had done.

He lies unmoving in the half-light. His body feels bruised and bloated, like a piece of flotsam tumbled roughly by the tide. He knows that he has felt release in Lulu's arms, and the idea terrifies him. He looks at Lulu now with amazement. He sees the cropped head of boyish hair, the thin line of lips, the flat rise of his chest, and the thickly calloused palms of his upturned hands. Nathan feels nothing now, no remaining vestige of desire. Instead he feels only shock at what has transpired. He cannot imagine the feel of those lips upon his own, and cannot fathom the tow of longing that brought him here in the first place. His mind eases slightly. I am normal, he thinks. A man like any other.

Slowly he rises and slips from the bed. He finds his tamer's clothes upon the floor and pulls them on, taking care not to make a sound. But as he moves to leave he hears a stirring in the bed, and when he turns he sees Lulu watching him apprehensively. Nathan freezes, and the two men stare at each other.

'I must go,' says Nathan.

'To where?' asks Lulu.

'The lions will need tending.'

'Will you return?' Lulu lifts his chin a little defiantly, as if to guard himself against Nathan's response.

Nathan hesitates, unable to bear the look of hope mixed with alarm in Lulu's eyes. 'I do not think so,' he says quietly. He lowers his head.

'Are you certain?'

'Yes.'

'How can you be?' Lulu's tone is unyielding.

Nathan pauses. He cannot be certain of anything.

'Perhaps you might,' says Lulu when he does not answer. 'Perhaps you might return.' His voice fades on the last word, loses its authority.

'Perhaps,' murmurs Nathan, his voice barely rising above a whisper. And then he turns to go.

41
Lulu

FOR SOME TIME after – he does not know if it is
minutes or hours – Lulu remains motionless in the
vast mahogany bed. It is his most expensive posses-
sion, and he likes to think the flamboyant curl of the
headboard is worthy of kings. It took him two years to save
the money to buy the bed, and he often lingers upon it late
into the afternoon. It is more than just a place to sleep: it is a
refuge and a comfort, and a vehicle for his dreams.

Last night his dreams came briefly true, but the cost to
Lulu is more than he can bear. He wishes he had not
stumbled on to Nathan in the dark outside the tent. He'd
have been content with only distant possibilities. Now he is
left only with the knowledge that he has found the cage boy
and lost him in the space of a night.

For Lulu *had* found him, he feels convinced of this. Last
night he had looked into the boy and glimpsed the fragile
core of his spirit. The boy's vulnerability, his isolation, his
uncertainty – Lulu had never permitted himself such things.

They were much too dangerous for a boy who dressed as girls. But they were not unfamiliar.

So it wasn't just the cage boy's beauty. There was more to it than lust. It was like an infestation from which Lulu could not rid himself, for he had tried. The boy was lost, that much was clear. He needed anchoring. The way he'd clung to Lulu's shoulder; the way his grip did not relax until he'd fallen deeply into sleep. He was holding on to something. Lulu could only hope that it was him.

42

Nathan

WHEN NATHAN EMERGES from Lulu's flat, he is startled by the grey-brown haze that hangs about the air. It is almost noon, but the street outside is bathed in an eerie semi-darkness, as if a winter storm is imminent, but it is merely a blanket of dark fog, trapped by low-lying clouds. The temperature has plummeted during the night, and the cold air is deathly still. Nathan has not seen the sun in weeks and longs for it. He wonders how long people can survive without it. It is both a gift and a curse, he thinks, man's endless ability to adapt. Is this not what he did last night?

He begins the long walk home, heading south towards Trafalgar Square, his face lowered against the foul air. He allows the cold to seep into his body, for he wishes to be numb. His mind overflows with images from the previous evening. He should feel shame for his actions, but instead he feels regret. The world seems oddly brittle, as if the ground might crack beneath him and swallow him whole. Most of all, he is haunted by the look of betrayal on Lulu's face when he fled.

Nathan walks slowly, and as he does the dirty yellow fog seems to swell and envelop him. He moves through it like a ghost, and by the time he reaches Trafalgar Square it is so dense that he can barely see five paces in front of him. He hears the tower at Westminster strike twelve. It is Sunday morning and the streets are unusually quiet, as if people are afraid to venture out into the shrouded air. The gas lamps remain lit along the main thoroughfares, as if in acknowledgement of the danger that lurks around them. And when Nathan finally reaches the Embankment, he sees that the fog has finally hit some invisible obstacle and rolled itself into a great, lowering mass. For the first time he is nearly overcome: panic rises in him like the crest of a wave. He raises a sleeve to his face and tries to inhale the moist fibres of the wool instead of the dense fumes that surround him.

As he steps on to the bridge he can see nothing on the other side, and he must trust that Lambeth and its swamplands still remain. He thinks anxiously of Queen and Nero and the cubs and is relieved when, halfway across the bridge, he sees an end to the fog. He glances back with disbelief at the heavy cloud and wonders whether it is not an omen of some kind. Or perhaps, he thinks with regret, an admonishment.

He hurries along to Lambeth Walk, anxious to return to the company of animals. When he finally reaches the menagerie, Nero seems relieved to see him. He snarls a greeting and paces back and forth eagerly in his temporary enclosure, rubbing his sides against the bars. Nathan enters the cage and strokes him for a moment, before filling his water bowl and strewing a few handfuls of clean straw across the floor. He will clean the cage properly once Nero has been fed, but he is anxious first to check on Queen.

He approaches her cage quietly and peels back the sail-cloth so as not to disturb her and the cubs. It takes a moment for his eyes to find her in the darkness. She lies stretched along the ground on the far side of the wooden box, her back to him. She does not rise to greet him. He glances round the cage for the tiny cubs, noticing the absence of any sound. Perhaps they too are sleeping, tired from the ordeal of their birth.

And then he sees them in the corner, half-buried in the straw: their bodies oddly stiffened in the gloom. The sight is like a slap. Nathan stands frozen in the doorway, wondering whether he dare enter the cage. He rattles the padlock loudly, but Queen does not stir. For a split second he wonders whether she too is dead, but then he sees the lazy flick of her tail, as it rises once and falls upon the floor.

Slowly he eases the cage door open and steps inside. He stands for several moments, then crosses over to the corner where the cubs are. He crouches down and picks up the first. It is little bigger than his own hand and oddly formed. Its skin is like paper-thin velvet, and is mottled with dark spots. The cub appears half-wasted, its tiny body already stiff with death. Its eyes are tightly closed. The cub is still covered with the muck of birth, now dark and hard. It must have been born dead, he thinks, for surely Queen would not have left it in this state, had it been born alive. The feel of the dead cub in his hand repels him and he gingerly replaces it in the straw. He reaches down beneath it to retrieve the second cub, whose head is just visible peeking through the straw. But as he pulls it forth he gags, for though the cub's upper half is perfectly formed, its lower half is crushed and badly mauled, its bloody entrails hanging limply from a rupture in its hide. Horrified, he drops it in the straw. Its eyes are just open, lightly glazed with death, and its tiny front legs are splayed at an awkward angle, but its body is free from muck. Nathan knows this cub was born alive: he heard its tiny cries last night just before he went into the ring.

Queen remains immobile on the far side of the box. He cannot fathom why she would have killed the cub. Perhaps, he thinks, she could not bear to bring a cub into the world of men. Or perhaps she knew the cub was weak and would not live. Nathan stares at the furrowed ridge of Queen's spine and feels only desolation.

He glances down at the two dead cubs. He should remove them from the cage at once, but he cannot bring himself to act. He feels the hot salt of despair well up inside him, and the pile of straw and tiny bodies begin to swim before his eyes. He turns and sees Talliot wheel his mother through the doorway of the tent. Nathan wipes his eyes and backs out of the cage. Talliot pushes his mother to within a few feet of him. She gives a brief nod of her head, indicating that he should go, and Talliot seems relieved to do so. Nathan thinks of his drunken performance the night before, and wonders whether his mother has come to fire him. Instead she wheels herself over to the bars of the enclosure and nods towards Queen.

'Have you seen them?' she asks.

Nathan hesitates before replying. 'The cubs are dead,' he says.

His mother's face darkens. She stares into the cage, blinking rapidly. 'How many were there?'

'Only two.'

She frowns.

'One was born dead,' he says. 'She killed the other.' He can hear the tremor in his voice and hates himself for it.

She shrinks back in the chair, as if to distance herself from this new information. She holds herself rigid, but he can see the steady twitch of a tiny muscle in her jaw. 'It was her first litter,' she says, her voice cracking. 'Such things are not unheard of. It is a pity, but she'll recover.' She wheels her chair round to face Nero, who is pacing back and forth within his temporary cage.

'Nero is anxious without Queen,' Nathan's mother says, her voice calmer now. 'You may as well return him to the cage. And take down the sailcloth. The sooner she returns to work, the better. If we leave her too long, she may turn on us when it's time to go back in the ring. Do you understand?'

Nathan nods, thinking of the half-mauled cub lying in the straw. She has said nothing about his drunkenness; evidently she has decided not to fire him. He cannot help but wonder why. She seems anxious now to leave, wheeling herself over to the doorway and calling impatiently for Talliot. After a few moments he appears and pushes her away, leaving Nathan alone with Queen and Nero, and the debris of their offspring.

Nathan gazes at the two tiny cubs. For a moment, he thought his mother might break down. His mind hurtles back in time. Suddenly he is a tiny child standing in the brittle grass of the prairie, the hot winds of summer buffeting his face. The grass is so tall that he can barely see ahead of him, but still he can hear his mother's voice, a long, low, angry moan that makes his chest hurt. He pushes through the grass, the brittle stalks grazing his face and elbows, and sees a flicker of dark clothing. Instinctively, he pauses, then takes a few cautious steps forward. That is when he sees her. She is sitting, her knees drawn up tightly to her chest, her head tucked against them. He sees her body rock slowly back and forth, and the tall tips of grass around her move softly with the motion. His mother is swaying by herself in a field, and he does not know why. He glances behind him. Perhaps he should go and find the others. Or perhaps he should go to her, wrap his arms round her neck, and try to comfort her somehow.

But he does neither. He is afraid to move, so he remains hidden in the grass. He can feel the late afternoon sun beating down upon the back of his neck, and the sting of his own tears welling up in his eyes. His throat is dry and he wishes that he had stayed behind in the cool shadow of the wagon. Eventually, when he can stand it no longer, he lowers himself slowly to the ground. He makes a small space for himself at the base of the grass and curls up in a ball. After a few minutes, the heat lulls him into sleep.

Some time later, he wakes to the sound of his mother shouting for him in the distance. He sees that dusk has fallen, and rises unsteadily to his feet, rubbing his face with the palms of his hands. His arms and legs feel sore and scratchy from the grass. He hears his mother's voice again, this time a little closer, and begins to move towards it. It takes a minute to find her, and when he does, her face is taut with anger. She crosses the distance between them in three quick strides and grabs him by the shoulders, shaking him until his head hurts. When she asks where he's been, he does not know what to say. He stares at her mutely, and wishes he could forget what he has seen. Finally, she takes him by the hand and leads him towards the wagon. He sees her glance back to the long grass, as if it hides something evil.

43

Nan

WHILE NATHAN TENDS to Queen and the cubs, Nan stands uncertainly outside a house in Rotherhithe, her hands clenched in her armpits. She has come in search of Shad, but it is not too late to change her mind. She looks around her desperately. It took her nearly two hours to find her way here in the fog, though it should have taken half that time. She has been here only once before, though the street is firmly etched in her mind. The house belongs to the mother of a sailor Shad met at sea, and when he turned up on the doorstep with a letter from her son, she invited him to stay on.

Shad brought Nan here the other night, and when the old woman raised her candle to peer at them in the darkness of the doorway, he threw an arm about her shoulder.

'My sister Nan,' he beamed proudly. 'Come from Plymouth just today.'

The old woman's eyes flickered back and forth between them for a moment, and then she nodded and motioned them inside. Nan could see that she was half mad with age and solitude. The tiny house was crammed with gaudy paper ornaments and cheap tin trinkets that caught the light of her candle. They covered every grimy surface and even dangled from the ceiling, so that you had to duck beneath them to move about. Nan looked around in awe. The old woman must have spent a lifetime amassing them. As she stepped into the room, Nan heard a shuffling of paper and turned to see a flick of movement near the sideboard. She threw a glance at Shad, who raised an eyebrow.

After a few moments, the old woman nodded good night to them and slowly climbed the stairs to her bedroom, leaving them below. As soon as they heard the latch on her door, Shad took her by the hand and pulled her to the stairs. She stopped him.

'No, Shad. We mustn't. Not here.'

'Why not? She likes me,' he whispered. 'She's not seen her son for three years.'

Nan frowned. But by then Shad was already pulling her up the narrow flight of stairs and into the spare room, where a small wooden bed sat against the middle of the wall. Nan looked around. Except for the bed, the room was empty.

'Where are his things?'

Shad shrugs. 'With him, I guess.' Nan felt a twist of sadness for the old woman and her absent son. And then Shad was behind her, with his arms winding tightly round her waist.

Now she gazes up and down the tiny row of cottages. She is certain she has found the right road, though she cannot see further than twenty paces. She can hear the voices of children playing nearby, their bodies lost in the fog. She takes a deep breath and knocks upon the door. There is a rustling, and the door opens a few inches. She recognises the old woman at once: her small, crinkled eyes stare out at Nan with surprise.

'If you please, I've come for Shad,' she says hastily. 'It's his sister, Nan.' The old woman looks at her, and for a moment Nan wonders whether Shad has moved on. And then the old woman pushes the door open wide. Nan steps across the threshold. As she does the old woman wheezes loudly and begins to cough.

Nan steps closer to her, and when the old woman lays a bony hand upon her arm, Nan is startled by the firmness of her grasp. The coughing subsides after a few moments and the old woman points with the other hand to the room upstairs.

'Asleep,' she manages to say. Nan peers up into the darkness of the stairwell, and hears movement from above. Shad appears at the top of the stairs, his face swollen with sleep. Slowly he descends the stairs.

'Your sister, Shad,' wheezes the old woman. She turns back to Nan, nodding. 'I'd have baked a cake, had I known.'

'I'm sorry,' she murmurs. She looks at Shad with desperation.

'We'll walk out,' he says hastily. 'Won't we, Nan?'

She nods. The old woman frowns. Nan can almost feel her disappointment, but she cannot bear the cluttered room and its contents any longer. 'We'll leave you to your Sabbath,' she says then.

They walk out into the fog. As the door shuts behind them, Nan turns to him.

'You mustn't stay on there, Shad.'

'Why not?' He looks at her defiantly.

She cannot think of a reason. Shad takes a step forward and raises a hand to her face. At once, she pulls back, turning her head to one side.

'Don't.'

He glares at her. Just then they hear the shouts of children. They come bolting like horses out of the fog, career wildly past them, then disappear again.

'Let's go somewhere,' she says.

'Where?'

'Somewhere we can talk.' She looks around in despair. It is a problem that has always dogged them: the absence of a place where they belong.

'Come on,' he says, and takes her hand, pulling her along.

He threads her through the streets to the river, to a desolate-looking pub surrounded by warehouses. They sit upon a wooden bench outside, and Nan stares out at the swirling, murky currents of the Thames. She thinks of her father and Shad's mam and baby Fleur swimming just beneath the surface. She turns to Shad, and sees the fierce expression of longing on his face. It is a look that has haunted her all her life.

'I don't want to run away from you any longer,' she says resolutely. 'I want you to let me go.'

Shad looks at her and narrows his eyes. 'They left me to you,' he says slowly. 'Both of them. They trusted you.' He speaks of their mothers. The idea appals her.

'I never asked for their trust, Shad. I never wanted it.' She does not say the obvious: that she never wanted him.

Shad leans towards her, until his face is only a few inches from her own. 'You gave yourself to me,' he whispers hotly.

Nan feels herself colour. She looks away. 'That was a mistake,' she says.

Shad glares at her. 'There's no such thing,' he says fiercely.

They sit in silence and, try as she might, Nan cannot conjure a way forward. Even if he agrees to let her go, the very fact of him will dog her to the end. Shad was right: their mothers are to blame. It is as if they have been shackled to each other from the start.

He sits slouched beside her on the bench, chewing resolutely on his thumbnail. A ship slowly steams by, and Shad lifts his head to watch it pass. At length he speaks, his voice glum.

'Are you in love with the flyer?'

Nan looks at him and for a moment cannot follow his meaning. Then it dawns on her and she laughs. 'No,' she says emphatically, shaking her head.

He looks at her earnestly. 'He's a poof, you know. He likes his own.'

'Oh stop it, Shad.'

'You don't believe me, do you?' he says defensively. Nan rolls her eyes in response. 'I know. I've seen him.'

She turns to him crossly. 'You followed him?'

He shrugs, then nods.

She shakes her head in dismay. 'Oh, Shad, you are completely daft.'

'I've seen him with the tamer, Nan. I've seen them together.'

'What do you mean?' she asks slowly.

Shad senses he has hit upon something, though he is not sure what. 'The lion tamer,' he says. 'I saw them. Just last night.'

Nan stops breathing. She stares at him in mute surprise.

'They're all margeries, Nan. The whole bloody lot of them.'

In her mind Nan sees Nathan and Lulu together: sees their two young bodies entwined. She feels her chest tighten.

Shad is not fool enough to mistake the look upon her face. Once again he leans in close, and drops his voice to a whisper.

'We've all got our soft spots, Nan. I guess I just found yours.'

44

The Lions

QUEEN WATCHES THE cage boy remove the large strips of sailcloth that have blighted her life for the past two days, together with the soiled wooden box, which she now refuses to enter. The boy moves silently and will not meet her gaze. She wonders why he does not greet her in his usual way, wonders why he does not kneel beside her and run his warm hands along the curve of her spine. However, she knows that nothing is the same in the cage. The mouldy sheets of sailcloth, the dirty wooden box, the dishevelled pile of straw in the corner: these things have altered the cage for ever. Even after he has taken them from her sight, Queen knows that she will not be free of them.

But where are the cubs? She feels confusion at their absence, and irritation, for the teats along her belly are now fat with milk. Every hour the pressure increases, and she yearns for relief. Perhaps the boy can help her, though she does not know how. She raises herself up to a sitting position, and shifts round to face him as he goes about his tasks.

But he does nothing. The cage is empty now, except for Nathan and herself, and he stands silently, facing the empty corner where the straw had been. In his hand is a broom, which hangs loosely by his side. He stands frozen in a manner that reminds her of the zebras on the veldt, who try to conceal themselves simply by remaining still. But after several moments, he can hold his pose no longer, and his shoulders begin to shake in tiny movements. Queen watches as the features of his face contort, sees his tightly closed eyes overflow. The sight alarms her.

She would like to cross the cage, to move in close and rub her silken fur against the sides of his legs, to soothe him in the only way she can, but she does nothing. Something prevents her, as if she is tethered to the floor. Instead she can only watch as the boy begins to sob, his breath coming in strangled gasps. The sound unnerves her. She feels the heat rise within her and the thirst return. She gives an enormous shake of her head to free herself from the tangled images in her brain, but to no avail. At that moment, the milk releases again inside her. The flesh of her teats swells so tight she fears that they will burst. She shakes her head again. When she stops, she sees the boy is no longer crying, and has turned his face to gaze at her. She knows the look in his eyes from her former life on the veldt. The boy wears the face of the wounded.

45
Nan

NAN SITS ALONE in the darkness in the back row of the tent. Below her, the equestrienne twins practise endlessly in the ring. It is a new stunt, one she has never seen before, in which one rider jumps through a wooden hoop held aloft by the other, both moving in opposite directions round the ring. The stunt requires split-second timing, and the twins attempt it more than two dozen times before they succeed. Nan watches in fascination, for she has never before appreciated the monotony of their task. Over and over they practise the trick, their faces thick with concentration, as if the world outside the ring has ceased to exist. Nan is impressed by their dedication, but feels that they are flawed. There is something vaguely inhuman about their obsessive quest for perfection. They eat and sleep and breathe their vocation. But without their horses, what would they be?

Her eyes move to the wooden crate at her feet. She has been sitting high up in the darkness for nearly three hours, ever since her talk with Shad. She will have to move down soon, for the show is little more than an hour away.

The twins finish rehearsing and lead the horses back to the stables. A groom begins to sweep the ring in preparation for tonight's performance, and Nan watches as Talliot enters the ring to give instructions to the groom, before disappearing down the passage to the menagerie. She wonders whether Nathan has arrived, and whether she will have the courage to face him, for she does not know what to make of Shad's words. Perhaps she should leave, take her oranges and her pride and flee this place.

Instead she goes in search of Lulu. Backstage, the performers have begun to arrive and ready themselves for the show. Nan sees the equestriennes applying each other's make-up, their too-broad faces still shiny from exertion. The clowns, already in full costume, have compressed themselves into a tiny corner at the back. There are normally three, but tonight Nan sees that only two have arrived. Each holds a tiny dog in his lap, fully grown but no bigger than the span of a man's hand. The dogs form part of the act and the clowns fondle them like children. Indeed, Nan thinks that they are treated better than most children, kept on scraps of bread and gammon bones. Nan watches as the dogs whine and yelp and lash their tiny tails, begging for more food. The clowns hold the morsels above them, urging the dogs to jump higher each time. Nan realises she has not eaten since dawn.

She goes to Lulu's dressing room and knocks gently upon the door. Lulu calls for her to enter, and Nan sees that something is amiss. Lulu greets her with an odd half-smile but his face is pinched and pale, and the whites of his eyes are streaked with red. He has yet to put on his hairpiece, and has begun to slick his own hair back with oil, so that the corners of his cheekbones appear even more pronounced than usual.

Lulu looks at his reflection in the mirror, then smiles up at Nan. 'Sometimes the flesh cannot be transformed,' he says weakly. Nan manages a small smile in return, but can think only of Shad's words. She watches as Lulu begins to apply make-up to his cheeks. He puts it on thicker than he should in an effort to conceal what lies beneath, but the result appears garish.

'Are you all right?' she asks finally.

Lulu purses his lips. 'I am,' he says. Nan sees his fingers tremble slightly as he wipes a slash of blue across his eyelids. Then he picks up a brush and slowly begins to paint his lips bright red with cochineal. When he finishes, he purses his lips together, then frowns at the result. His eyes dart up to Nan's reflection.

He sighs. 'A lover's quarrel, nothing more,' he says.

Lulu motions for her to hand him a towel hanging on a hook by the door, and as Nan reaches for it, she comes face to face with Nathan. Nathan's eyes move past her to Lulu. Nan looks from one man to the other, and knows with certainty that something has transpired between them. The colour drains from Nathan's cheeks, and he lowers his head, as if her gaze is more than he can bear.

'Forgive me,' he murmurs. As he turns away and disappears down the corridor to the menagerie, Nan slowly turns back to Lulu. He remains immobile in front of the mirror.

'For what does he apologise?' she asks.

Lulu's eyes briefly meet hers, then swivel back to his reflection in the mirror. 'I wish I knew,' he says, his voice nearly swallowed by despair.

46

Nathan

THE FOLLOWING DAY, Nathan finds himself outside the rundown gin palace by Vauxhall Station. The dense fog that smothered the West End has begun to lift, though a shroud of dirty residue still hangs about the Thames. For the second time he climbs the dingy brown stairs, and knocks at the door. The same gruff voice shouts for him to enter, and when he does, Nathan recognises Stickley at once. He stands nervously in front of the massive wooden desk, while Stickley scrutinises him from head to toe.

'I know you. You're the cage boy.'

Nathan nods. 'Yes, sir.'

Stickley gestures towards the room's only other chair. Nathan seats himself, relieved that the man and his office, at least, are exactly as he remembers.

'I've seen you perform. You've got a bright future, if you want it.' He slams the ledger shut in front of him and leans back in his chair, folding his arms across his chest. Nathan feels himself colour, for he is unused to praise. Stickley shifts forward in his chair and eyes him. 'What brings you back to me, then?'

Nathan pulls the folded playbill from his pocket and spreads it out on the desk in front of him, smoothing the page with his palms. Stickley frowns.

'I need to know more about her,' Nathan says quietly.

Stickley raises his eyebrows in surprise. 'Why?'

Nathan hesitates. 'I used to know her. In the mud circus. A long time ago.'

Stickley squints at him. 'How old did you say you were?'

'Nineteen.'

Stickley frowns. 'You've got a good memory, lad. 'Cause she's been over here for fifteen years.'

Nathan nods slowly, but says nothing.

Stickley pulls a matchbox from his pocket and lights a match, cupping the flame to the stub of his cheroot. He sucks in hard several times, exhaling smoke with each breath, and the spiced aroma blankets the room. Stickley levels his gaze at Nathan.

'What is it you wish to know?' he asks finally.

Nathan nods towards the playbill. 'Why did you warn me off her?'

Stickley shrugs. 'I only meant . . . do your job and keep your nose clean. She's not one to hold with wastrels.'

'That I know,' says Nathan. He waits for Stickley to continue.

'She's an odd sort of woman,' he says then, puffing on his cheroot.

Nathan shifts uneasily. 'How long have you known her?'

'Years. Since her heyday. About the time this was taken.' He indicates the photograph.

'Was she famous?'

'In her time. She wasn't the best rider in London, mind you. But she was a grand performer. Knew how to hold an audience, keep them on the edge of their seats. And she had the looks in those days. My God, she had the looks of an angel. Men used to pay double for the front row.' He draws on the cigar, then blows the smoke out into the room. 'Of course the accident changed all that.'

'What happened?'

'She rode too hard. She was ambitious. And equestriennes were plentiful in those days. You had to fight to earn your place. But she wanted it all, wanted the crowd at her feet.' Stickley removes the cigar from his mouth and studies it a moment, before carefully stubbing it out in a small china saucer. He licks his fleshy lips before continuing. 'The night she fell, she'd done three shows in one day, and it was her last time round the ring. The stage was smaller than what she was used to, and the horse was tired. I was backstage and I could see her urging him on for the final jump. They came around towards me, and I remember seeing the horse's eyes roll right back in its head. I remember thinking: Christ Almighty, he's finished. And in the next instant they both went down, and the horse rolled over her. Just like that.' He drops a meaty hand down upon the table with a thud. 'She was lucky to survive. But her career was finished.'

'What happened to her then?'

'Well, there was still her husband's career to manage. He was very famous in those days. Much more than her, so she was kept busy, after a fashion. They had a kind of partnership. Never signed a contract without the other. And always went on tour together. Rumour had it, she wouldn't let him out of her sight when they were abroad.'

Nathan frowns. 'Was he unfaithful?'

At this, Stickley guffaws. 'Not likely. He was a trainer through and through. He lived for the animals. Nothing else much mattered to him.'

Nathan hesitates. 'What about her?' he asks. 'Did she matter?'

Stickley shrugs and raises his eyebrows. 'That's an odd sort of question. Who knows what goes on between a man and his wife?' He pauses, frowning. 'But something happened between the two of them after the accident. She couldn't travel any more, on account of the chair. So she persuaded him to settle in London, and invest in his own show. I partnered with them for a time, together with Talliot, and a few others. It was a grand show, and for a while we gave the likes of the Alhambra a run for its money.'

'So what happened?'

'Two things. There was a bad fire and we were forced to close for six months. We lost a lot of our stock, and nearly half the animals, and it took time before we could raise enough funds to replace them. Jack was under considerable pressure at the time, because the Americans had begun to pay huge sums for circus animals and we couldn't compete with their prices. When he finally struck a deal, he had to train the new cats up as fast as possible, in order that we could reopen and recoup our losses.'

'What was the other?'

Stickley purses his lips together, as if unwilling to speak. 'Mad Jack had a rival in those days, an African called Macomo. He was a giant of a man, nearly seven foot tall, with skin as black as tar. And unlike most tamers, he was teetotal. Never touched a drop of spirits, and never swore. The lions feared him, but they respected him as well. You could see it in their eyes when he performed.

'Anyway, Macomo introduced the idea of "lion-hunting" in the ring. It was a sensational act, and audiences flocked to see him. He would chase the animals about the cage, armed with a sword and pistols, and mimic a real hunt. It could only be done with younger animals. The older ones wouldn't be driven and hustled in that way. But it was a huge success and, for a time, he drew the biggest crowds in all of Europe. He and Jack were friends of a sort. All right, they was rivals in the ring, but it was always amicable, and the two men respected each other. In truth, I don't think Jack was much bothered by Macomo's popularity.' He pauses and leans forward, nodding towards the playbill on his desk.

'But she was. As soon as we reopened after the fire, she persuaded us to stage a sort of competition. Two shows simultaneously, side by side, in separate oval cages. She was convinced that if people saw both men perform together, they'd be persuaded that Jack was the better tamer of the two. The idea was that after the show, the audience would be allowed to vote on the winner, and the one who was chosen would be lion king for the season.

'Well, the idea went down well enough at first. Both men agreed in principle. But then the trouble started. She wanted them to try something big, something that would cause a bit of a sensation. And she got it in her head that for the act's finale, they should stage a double bounce. Now the bounce is no ordinary lion trick. Only a handful of tamers have ever managed it. And not every lion will do it. The tamer puts two lionesses into a small, rectangular cage and, working from the outside, stirs them up into a frenzy. When they're ready, he rushes into the cage. A nervous lioness, when confronted in a small cage, will fly outwards towards the bars, and then upwards. With a bit of training, she'll take off into the air and go round and round the bars six feet up, as if she's flying. The tamer stands in the middle as the lions hurl around him. He looks as if he's on the brink of death. It's a grand trick, one that sweeps the crowd every time. But it takes total concentration, and split-second timing on the part of the tamer. And no one had ever tried it in tandem.

'Macomo was dead against it, and even Jack was doubtful. They were worried that each cage would be distracted by the animals in the other. But she worked on them until they agreed. They practised for a few weeks in advance, and things seemed to go well enough in rehearsals. But both men were uneasy.

'On the eve of the show, Macomo called us all together and said his cats weren't behaving well at all. He wanted to drop the bounce from the finale. Jack was of a similar mind, but she wouldn't hear of it. She said both men had signed a contract, and that a lot of money had been put up for publicity, and that if they cancelled, they'd lose both the audience and the show's investors for good. She said it was the chance of a lifetime, and I remember the silence in the room after she'd spoken.'

He pauses and takes a deep breath. When he exhales, Nathan can smell the remnants of cigar smoke, mixed with the sour smell of ale. Stickley shrugs. 'But who were we to oppose her? We needed to recoup our losses, and let me tell you, in those days, audiences loved the idea of a tamer going straight from the circus to the morgue. Anyway, Macomo was right: we should never have gone through with it.' He shakes his head ruefully, and for the first time Nathan sees the guilt in his face. Stickley stares at his hands for a few seconds before continuing.

'Mad Jack used to say that the first two minutes of an act would make or break it, because the animals are always agitated when they first enter the ring. Well, that night, as soon as the act had begun you could see that something wasn't right. Macomo's lead cat was sluggish and sour-tempered. Twice in the first few minutes, Macomo had to stop the act to discipline it. I could see Macomo wasn't happy, but he persevered, and halfway through the act he seemed to relax a little, 'cause things were going better. And then it came time for the finale. He got them going all right, but when he rushed the cage, his lead cat turned on him. Well, Macomo held his ground. He had a hell of an imposing figure, and when he swung a whip it made us all jump, I can tell you. But he was so focused on the lead cat, he forgot about the other. He turned his back on it for a second, and it jumped him. Before you could blink the lead cat was on him too. The cage was nothing but a storm of teeth and fur. Macomo tried to fight them off with the whip, but he was down from the start.

'Of course we were in there in a flash. We shot the lead cat dead, and the other fell away soon enough. But Macomo took a bad mauling. His injuries were horrific. He lost the lower half of his arm that night, and one eye. I'll never forget the look of astonishment upon his face when he was carried out of the cage. It was like he'd been betrayed, but I never knew who he blamed. The animals or her.'

Stickley swallows and the look upon his face is terrible. 'He died four days later in hospital, after the infection had taken hold. Mad Jack was devastated. He wasn't the same in the ring after that, and his career fell into decline. And the marriage – well, I expect it was as good as over the day Macomo died. I don't think Jack ever forgave her.' Stickley pauses, looking down at his hands splayed upon the desk.

'How did he die?' asks Nathan.

'Who, Jack?' Stickley looks at Nathan and frowns. 'He hanged himself. Two years later. They found his body swinging from the ceiling of the cage one morning. The lions never even touched his carcass. Just let him hang there. And no one had the guts to cut him down. They were afraid the cats would turn on them if they tried.' Stickley shakes his head. 'Let me tell you something, son. We're all cowards in this business. We pay people a pittance to risk their lives in the ring, but we wouldn't stick our own necks out for all the money in the world. That's the truth of it.'

'She told me that he lost his nerve,' Nathan says.

Stickley narrows his eyes. 'Maybe he did, though it wasn't the cats he was afraid of. I think, in the end, she drove him to despair. But he couldn't bring himself to leave her, on account of the chair. So he did the only other thing that he could do. Which was worse, of course. Another kind of parting.' He pauses for a moment. 'We were all stunned by his death, but none so much as her. For her, it was the end of everything.'

Nathan stares at him. 'She had a son in America.'

Stickley raises his eyebrows in surprise. Nathan sees a flicker of doubt cross his face. 'Now how do you know that?'

Nathan hesitates. 'We were kids together,' he says. 'Her boy and me. Like brothers almost.'

Stickley eyes him uncertainly, weighing his words. 'Well, I never knew a thing about a child,' he says slowly.

'She never spoke of him?'

Stickley shakes his head. 'Not in my company. But then, it's not the kind of thing you'd go shouting from the rooftops, now is it?'

Nathan frowns. 'I suppose not.'

Stickley leans forward. 'Did you ask her?'

Nathan nods. 'She told me he was dead.'

'Too bad for her.'

Nathan hesitated. 'But I don't believe her.'

'Why would she lie?'

'I don't know.'

Stickley shakes his head. 'She was hardly the sort to mother a child.'

Nathan feels himself grow hot. 'I guess not,' he says, his voice dropping to a whisper.

Stickley softens his tone. 'Is that why you came all this way, to find her son?'

Nathan feels a lump rise in his throat. He nods, unable to speak.

'Well, I'm sorry I couldn't help you.'

Nathan rises to his feet.

The older man looks at him expectantly. 'You'll stay on though, won't you?'

Nathan hesitates. 'I don't know.'

Stickley leans forward. 'Listen to me lad: you've only just begun.'

Nathan gives a weak smile. He does not know whether he is at the start of something, or the finish.

47

The Lions

NERO WATCHES HELPLESSLY as Queen chews and chews. The scent of blood is in his nostrils and confuses him, for it is Queen who bleeds. He knows better than to interrupt her, he can sense that she is in danger. She has not been the same since the cage boy reunited them yesterday evening. She will not meet his eye, and seems barely aware of his presence. Twice this morning he approached her to run his side along the length of her coat, but each time she moved as soon as he came near, neatly sidestepping his greeting. The second time he saw her ears and tail flatten, and the deadly curl of her upper lip against the white of her teeth. Instantly he retreated to the far side of the cage. She lay down, her back to him, her head resting lightly on her paws.

He must have dozed off. He does not know how long he slept, but when he woke, it was with a jarring sense of urgency. At once he was on his feet, but when he turned to look at Queen he saw that she was surrounded by a dark pool of blood. Her nostrils and jaw were smeared with red, and even the sides of her coat were spotted in places where she'd rubbed her face against herself. She was doubled over on herself, gnawing intently at something that he couldn't quite make out. He eased himself forward so as to get a better view, and when he did he saw that Queen had bitten off the end of her own tail. All that remained was a bloody stump of bone, and as he stood silently watching her she continued to chew, working her own flesh like it was the soft throat of an impala.

Now Nero closes his eyes but cannot sleep. The tent is colder than usual, and the chill irritates him. He wishes Queen would stop. He would like to work the ring with her again, would like to feel the smooth rub of her muscled shoulder against his own, would like to climb upon her back in a tight clench of desire. But nothing is the same inside the cage. Life outside seems to have altered as well. The cage boy appears tired and withdrawn. He no longer seems to take pleasure in performing, and does not fondle him the way he did. The others, too, are increasingly agitated. Even the old woman is more pinched and white than ever.

Nero feels the rumbling in his abdomen. The tent is strangely deserted today, for he has not seen a soul but Kezia since he woke. Twice this morning, the ageing orang-utan poked her head outside her wooden box to stare across the floor in Queen's direction. Nero could see her fear, and her helplessness. The sight made him even more uneasy. Like Kezia, he does not know what to do.

Where is the cage boy? Nero's stomach tells him he is late. Perhaps today is not a day of feeding, he thinks with alarm.

Every now and then, the cage boy appears and gives them only water and clean straw, though Nero doesn't understand why. Perhaps that is Queen's problem, he thinks desperately. Perhaps she is too hungry, and that is why she greedily devours her own flesh. But Nero knows this is not the case. He fears that whatever ails Queen is larger than a lump of horseflesh, and of far greater consequence.

48

Nan

NAN HAS COME to find Nathan. Last night he refused to look at her. He had performed badly, going about his routine like a sleepwalker, and even Nero had seemed wrong-footed by his mood. Twice the lion had almost missed his cue, but Nan could see that it was Nathan, not Nero, who had erred. Even before the act had ended, the audience had grown restless, shifting uneasily in their seats.

Lulu, too, had been affected. He emerged from his commode with swollen eyes, his face badly painted, and could manage only the barest of smiles as he climbed up the rope. Nan had caught a glimpse of Talliot standing in the wings, and had seen him frown when Lulu entered the ring. A few minutes later, she watched in horror as Lulu nearly missed the catch on his third stunt. Lulu caught the bar with only one hand, the force of his weight jerking the rope and spinning his body round in the air. A loud murmur of alarm went up from the crowd and, for a moment, Lulu seemed unable to right himself. He dangled for what seemed like an eternity, and for a moment Nan feared he might let go. Out of the corner of her eye, she saw Talliot lean forward in alarm. Then Lulu hoisted himself back on to the bar, and finished his act.

Now as she enters the menagerie, Nan is struck by the chill in the air. The coal fire has not been tended, a job Nathan normally sees to, and the animals are huddled deep in their straw beds in an effort to keep warm. She crosses to the iron stove and then she sees it: a mass of dark red surrounding Queen, who lies motionless on her side. Nero is buried in a pile of straw at the opposite corner of the cage, and Nan can see that he is not asleep, but watching her with a wary eye. She approaches the cage slowly, straining in the half-darkness to detect some sign of life from Queen. She circles round to where she can get a better view, and in that instant Queen raises her bloody head to look at her. Nan stares at Queen in horror, for the lioness's face is covered in a dark stain of dried blood and her eyes are glazed with mucus. Queen gazes at her, then lays her head upon the floor with a strangled cough. Nan looks quickly around the deserted tent. Nero continues to track her with one eye, and the orang-utan has poked her head out from her wooden box, but there is no other sign of life.

She hears a sound behind her, and turns to see Talliot push the old woman through the doorway of the tent. Both stare at her as if she has no business being there, and only after a moment do they see Queen lying in the pool of blood.

'Mother of God,' murmurs Talliot under his breath.

'What's happened here?' The old woman looks sharply up at Nan.

'I don't know,' she stammers. 'I only just came in.'

Talliot pushes the old woman cautiously towards the cage.

'There's been a fight,' says Talliot, glancing at Nero in disgust. 'He's killed her, that's what's happened.'

'No,' says the old woman. 'She's alive. Can't you see? But she will die soon if she continues to bleed like that.' She glances at Nan. 'Where is Nathan?'

Nan shakes her head. 'I don't know.'

'What are you doing here?' asks the old woman.

Nan hesitates. 'I came to find him.'

The old woman raises an eyebrow but says nothing. She looks Nan up and down, as if she is seeing her for the first time. Finally, she returns her attention to Talliot.

'We'll have to find him,' she says. 'Queen needs tending, and it's too great a risk for anyone else to enter the cage when this has happened.' Talliot nods and moves to take her chair, but she raises a hand to stay him. To Nan, they resemble royalty: an ageing queen and her long-suffering courtier. The old woman looks back at her and frowns.

'Perhaps we should ask you where Nathan can be found,' she says stiffly.

Nan squirms uncomfortably under her gaze. She can hear the animosity in the old woman's voice. She shakes her head, but in her mind she sees Nathan perched upon the bridge. The old woman stares at her unblinking for several moments, then motions for Talliot, and Nan watches as he wheels her out the door.

Twenty minutes later Nan has arrived, out of breath, at London Bridge. The bridge is crowded, for the day's workers have already begun their journey home, and the light is fading as the early winter dusk approaches. She struggles to see through the crowd, and eventually spots Nathan leaning up against the parapet on the far side of the bridge, his eyes on the water below. She makes her way across the bridge, realising as she draws near that he is completely oblivious to his surroundings. She lays a cold hand upon his arm.

'Nathan,' she says gently.

He gives a start, and it seems to Nan that he barely recognises her. His eyes fall to her hand upon his arm. At once she removes it.

'Nathan, there's trouble. You must come,' she says urgently.

'What is it?' he asks.

'It's Queen,' she says. 'Something's happened in the cage.'

He stares at her, then frowns, and turns back to the dark river running beneath them. 'Talliot will have to see to it,' he murmurs.

Nan stands watching him, for she has never before seen the troubled look upon his face. She does not know what to say. She had thought that the news of Queen would bring him running, and the idea that the lioness is of so little consequence to him puzzles her. Then she remembers Lulu.

'Nathan, what is wrong?'

He takes a deep breath of the cold evening air, then exhales slowly, and she watches as his breath rises out over the Thames, then disappears. 'Is it Lulu?' she asks tentatively.

Nathan turns to her, his expression guarded. 'No,' he says abruptly. He hesitates, evidently struggling with himself. 'What do you know of Lulu?'

Nan feels her heart race. 'I know that Lulu is unhappy. And that you are the cause.'

'I never meant to hurt Lulu,' he says quietly. Nan says nothing, and he turns back to the river with a sigh. 'I made a mistake,' he says finally. 'Have you never made a mistake?'

Nan thinks of her own catalogue of errors. 'Yes,' she whispers. She turns to look at the seething current beneath them. A longboat bobs by, its oarsmen pulling hard in the current, and a tug blows its shrill whistle as it crosses its path.

'Lulu is in love with you,' she says.

Nathan slowly shakes his head. 'I'm not the sort of person people fall in love with,' he replies.

Nan feels the anger mount within her. 'Don't be so sure,' she says hotly. Then she turns to go, leaving Nathan wide-eyed on the bridge behind her.

49

Nathan

NATHAN STANDS UPON the bridge watching Nan's retreating figure. All his life women have receded from him: first his mother, then Gina, and now Nan. He does not know what to make of her last words and must resist the tide of longing that rises up inside him like a great wave. Nathan closes his eyes: he must not succumb to loneliness.

His mind circles back to the eve of his departure. Riza appears in the grass outside his wagon, stamping his feet in the cold, his hands tucked beneath the armpits of his coat. Nathan is pleased to see him, though for some days he has been nervous at the prospect of their parting. Riza crouches down to enter. He can just manage to stand inside the wagon, though his bulky form fills up the tiny space. The strongman runs a thickened hand across the shiny pate of his head. His eyes drift across the neatly stacked piles of Nathan's belongings.

Then he notices the faded playbill lying unfolded on the

bed. He takes a step forward, and the muscles of his jaw tighten. Nathan feels a stab of regret that he's left the paper lying out. Riza clears his throat and turns away. He reaches inside his jacket and pulls out a small flask of whiskey.

'Let us drink to your departure.'

Nathan smiles. He does not share Riza's fondness for whiskey, but he is touched by the gesture. He clears a space on the bed for each of them to sit and fetches a pair of glass tumblers from the wagon's only shelf. Riza fills the glasses and hands one to Nathan, raising the other in a toast.

'To your future.'

Nathan sees the strongman's fingers tremble as he lifts the glass. For the first time, it occurs to him that Riza will be left alone when he is gone. The thought unsettles him.

'Riza, why do you not take a wife?'

The strongman looks at him with mock severity, then shakes his head vigorously. 'I am too old,' he says. 'And much too accustomed to the sound of my own voice. In fact, I prefer it.' He sets the glass down decisively on the small wooden table.

'We could find you someone quiet. A mime perhaps.'

Riza laughs. He reaches for the flask and refills his glass. 'Young Nathan, it's you who must marry. It's too late for me.'

Nathan frowns. 'There are many who would have you,' he says.

Riza raises an eyebrow. 'So you think. But not the right ones. Not the ones whose glance is like the bite of a snake.'

Nathan has never heard Riza speak of women in this way, and for a moment he is stunned.

'So you are not immune,' he says.

'What man is immune? There is no such immunity.'

'Did you never think of marrying?'

'Only once.'

'Giselle?'

Riza shakes his head. 'It was long ago. Before your time.'

'Who was she?'

'A performer, who else? A member of the tribe.' Riza smiles sheepishly.

'What happened?'

'She rejected my offer.' He pauses, and swallows a mouthful of whiskey. Then his expression grows more serious. 'She had a better one, it seems.'

'What was she like?'

Riza sucks in air, his enormous chest expanding until Nathan thinks that it will burst. His mouth is pressed in a tight line, and Nathan wonders if he has asked one question too many. But then the strongman exhales.

'She was angry. And passionate. And terrifying. And I could not get enough of her.' He gives a small, pained smile. Then he leans forward, wagging his index finger in the air. 'That is how it should be Nathan. Never settle for the other kind.'

Nathan looks at Riza and what he sees causes him almost to shrink back in alarm. He has always admired and respected the strongman. He does not want to think of him as somehow broken by his past. Perhaps that is what love does, he thinks, breaks us down, weakens us somehow, until we are no longer whole.

Riza reads the doubts in his mind. 'Do not be afraid to live, Nathan. Your mother would not have wanted that.'

'Who knows *what* my mother would have wanted,' Nathan says bitterly. 'One thing is for certain: she didn't want me.'

Riza frowns and shakes his head softly. 'You don't know this, Nathan.'

'But I can assume.'

'You can assume nothing!' Riza's voice has risen sharply, and his face is flushed with emotion. He looks down at his glass, and takes a deep breath. When he speaks again, his voice has softened. 'Until you stand in her shoes, you cannot know.' The two men stare at each other.

'Then I will find her,' says Nathan finally. 'And I will ask her face to face.'

'And then you will know,' says Riza. 'But not before, Nathan. Not before.'

Nathan stares down at the muddy water of the Thames. He has never understood why Riza chose to defend his mother at the moment of their parting. To his mind, there is no possible reason she could offer that would justify her actions. And yet, he has not done what he set out to do. He has not faced her with the question. And now he wonders if he ever will.

I must go to Queen, he thinks finally. For whatever else shifts and alters in his muddled life, the lions still remain. He turns and sets off in the fading winter light for Lambeth Walk, hurrying his pace as he goes. When he arrives, the menagerie is deserted, and he is sorry he did not come sooner. The sight of Queen lying in a pool of blood makes his own run cold. Queen lies motionless on her side, and her tail is a stump of blood and bone. Nero rises instantly to all fours and gazes at him with relief. He takes a few steps forward, and gives several sharp snarls of greeting. Queen twitches slightly in response, but otherwise she does not stir.

Quickly Nathan goes behind the bar where Walter keeps the wooden box of medical supplies. As he removes the box from beneath the counter and grabs a bottle of spirits, he remembers the stump of Walter's arm. The thought bolsters him. If men can survive the loss of their parts, he thinks, then so shall Queen. Slowly he draws open the door and steps into the cage. Nero comes towards him, and for a split second Nathan fears he will attack. Instead, Nero begins to rub his enormous head and shoulders against Nathan's legs. Nathan runs his hands along the lion's spine in a gesture of reassurance, and after a few moments Nero retreats again to the corner of the cage, and seats himself.

Nathan advances cautiously towards Queen. The lioness does not move as he approaches, but he sees the glint of her eye as she tracks him across the cage. He pauses just behind her and crouches down to the floor, where he waits for several seconds, allowing her to adjust to his presence. His heart is beating hard. He has not come near Queen since before the cubs were born, and does not know how she will respond to his touch. Slowly he reaches out a hand towards her spine, and as he makes contact she gives a start.

Queen's fur is thick with dried blood and the densely sweet smell of it makes Nathan's stomach roll uneasily. He moves his hand up towards her head, to the favoured place behind her ears, and begins to rub her, the blood sticky to his touch. He feels her soften beneath his fingers, feels the taut rope of her muscles begin to unwind, and she gives a long, plaintive moan that makes him want to weep. He shuffles round to face her. She raises her head, then draws herself weakly upright and blinks a few times in the half-light of the tent. Her luminous tawny eyes struggle to focus. Mucus dribbles from her nostrils and the sides of her jaw are blackened with blood. Queen gives an enormous sigh and the hot stench of her breath washes over him. For a second he is nearly overcome, for it is as if she draws him right inside her warm wound. After a moment, the effort of holding her head upright seems too much for her, and she lowers herself heavily back to the floor.

Nathan sets to work. Carefully, he washes the bloody stump of her tail with spirits and, although Queen flinches several times, she does not protest. When he is satisfied that the wound is clean, he binds it gently with a long strip of cloth, wrapping it round and round and securing it as tightly as he dares. Then he rises and leaves the cage, returning a moment later with a large basin of fresh water and a pile of rags. He mops up the blood as best he can and covers the floor with a clean bed of straw, then slowly begins to wash Queen's coat, dipping the rags again and again into the basin until the water is stained a deep crimson. When he is finished, he rubs her coat dry with a woollen horse blanket, the loose skin of her reclining form sliding underneath his hands. He refills the water basin and places it by her side. At first she takes no notice. Then she lifts her enormous head and slowly begins to drink, her great pink tongue lapping noisily at the water. Nathan watches with relief as she takes in fluid, as if she is sucking life back into herself.

Throughout all this, Nero watches patiently from the

corner. When Queen is finished, Nathan leaves the cage and goes in search of food for them both. He steps outside to the small shed behind the menagerie where the butchered horse-meat is delivered and, taking a small axe, hacks off several large hunks of meat and bone. He carries the food in a metal bucket back to the lions' cage. Nero devours his portion at once, but Nathan must force a handful of small chunks of meat between Queen's jaws. She manages to swallow only a few, then collapses heavily into sleep, and Nathan flings the remainder in Nero's direction. He gathers up the dirty rags and stuffs them into the bucket, then eases open the door of the cage. As he steps out, he sees Talliot pushing his mother into the tent. Nathan stands silently as Talliot wheels her across the tent, her gaze on him.

'We've been out searching for you,' his mother says in clipped tones. She nods towards the cage. 'Queen nearly bled to death in your absence,' she adds accusingly.

'I've cleaned and dressed the wound as best I can,' says Nathan. 'She should recover. As long as there is no more damage.' This last word seems to hang in the silence between them.

His mother stares at him, her mouth pressed tightly together in a line. She turns to Talliot. 'Leave us,' she says then. He hesitates, then leaves the tent. She watches him go, and turns back to Nathan.

'Where were you earlier?' she demands.

'I went to see Stickley.'

She narrows her eyes. 'Why?'

He hesitates. 'To tell him I was leaving.'

Now it is her turn to be silent. She wheels herself slowly

forward until she is only a few feet from where he stands. 'I took you in, and taught you everything I know. Is this how you repay me?'

He shakes his head. 'I can never repay all that you have done.'

'You could have been as good as he was. Better perhaps.'

'We're not the same.'

'You are more alike than you know,' she snaps.

Nathan feels his insides lurch.

'And what of the act?' she says, lifting her chin defiantly. 'What of them?' She indicates the lions with her head.

'You'll find someone else,' he says, his voice as flat as glass, for he is determined not to break beneath her gaze.

Her eyes fly about the tent, as if they are searching for an outlet for her anger. 'Where do you intend to go?' she asks.

'Back where I came from,' he answers.

She stares at him. 'You came from me,' she says. He sees her head begin to shake almost imperceptibly, as if her body cannot contain the force of her words. He looks at her, and it does not feel the way it should.

'Your place is here,' she says without blinking. 'With us.' Her entire body is quaking now. She does not even seem aware of it, does not try to stop the terrible trembling that has seized her.

'You left me,' he says, his voice low. She leans back in the chair, as if the words themselves are pressing on her. Slowly, the trembling eases, and Nathan sees only the rise and fall of her chest. He wonders if she will ever speak to him again.

When she does, her voice is calmer. It slices cleanly across the silence of the tent. 'A very long time ago, I made an error,' she says. 'You were the consequence.' She purses her lips and looks away, as if there is no more that she can offer.

'And so you made another,' he says angrily.

'If you prefer to think of it that way. Though I left you in good hands. Better ones, perhaps, than my own.'

'Did your husband even know of me?' he asks.

'No.'

'You did not tell him?'

She hesitated. 'No.'

'Why?'

'When I performed in America we were already betrothed. My husband had a contract touring Mexico at the time. But it was a wild, savage country, and he did not think it safe for a woman, so I took a job with the mud circus instead. He was a great success in Mexico. After eighteen months, he wrote to say that he had renewed his contract for another year. And then I did not hear from him for a very long time. As the months passed, I grew more and more fearful for his safety. After a time, I was convinced he was dead.'

She pauses for a moment and takes a deep breath. 'And then I met another man. I fell pregnant, and had a child. And though I was not the best of mothers, the child was the only thing that kept me going. And then, nearly two years later, my husband wrote to me. He said that he would leave for Europe in the following year, and that he would await my return.'

Nathan stares at her.

'I thought that I had lost him. And then I learned that he was still alive. I was not prepared to risk losing him again.'

'Not even for me?'

She hesitates. 'I was forced to make a choice.'

He stares at her for a long time. 'And afterwards, you had no other children?'

She frowns. 'I found that I could not.' Her voice trails off.

'And my father?'

She shrugs. 'Another performer. It does not matter now.'

'Perhaps not to you,' he says darkly. For all these years he has been obsessed by the memory of his mother. He has barely considered the identity of his father.

'I am surprised you do not know,' she says a little wearily, brushing a stray wisp of hair absently from her face. 'I thought perhaps that he would tell you. But then, I asked him not to.'

Nathan stares at her in stunned silence. He feels something drop like a weight inside him. 'Riza.'

His mother nods, eyeing him.

'He wanted to marry you.'

'Yes.'

'But you refused.'

'I did not love him.'

'You didn't love either of us.'

He sees her flinch. Then she lifts her chin and looks right at him, the lines of her neck taut.

'Not the way I loved him.'

Nathan feels his throat constrict. He turns away from her, his face hot, and crosses to the lion's cage, where he places both hands around the bars. He looks down at the knuckles of his hands, and is surprised by their tight, marbled whiteness. After a moment, he hears the wheels of his mother's chair move slowly across the ground. Her voice floats up behind him, the way it did the first time.

'I gave up everything for him,' she says with a faint trace of bitterness. 'More than he ever knew. In the end, I wished that I had told him.'

'I am more than just a measure of your love for your husband,' he says. 'Did you never even think of me?'

She hesitates. 'The day I left the mud circus was the day I lost you. It was as if you had perished.' She sighs. 'Nathan, you belong here. This is your home now. With us. With them.'

Nathan stares at the lions. Nero cleans himself obsessively, as if he is trying to purge himself of everything that has happened in the cage, while Queen continues to sleep. He does not turn round to face his mother.

'I don't know where my place is,' he says. 'But it isn't here with you.'

His eyes drop to the floor, scattered with sawdust, straw and dung. Behind him he can hear his mother's tightly measured breaths. All his life he has waited for this moment, but now he cannot bring himself to look at her. He hears the steady creak of wood, and the crush of straw against the floor. When he finally turns round to face his mother, she is gone.

He does not know how long he stands there: only that his throat is taut with emotion and his temple has begun to ache. He turns back towards the lions. It is true that he will miss them; she knows that much about him. He slides the cage door open and enters, going to where Queen lies. Slowly he eases himself down beside her sleeping form. He is suddenly unbearably tired, as if his body has been battered by his mother's words. He closes his eyes, and empties his mind. For tonight at least, he will sleep the sleep of lions.

Some time later, he is woken by a sound. He sits up in the cage, and lays a hand upon Queen's shoulder to check that she is breathing. The lioness is stretched out on her side, her bandaged tail jutting stiffly in the air. The tent is dark, but Nathan can just make out a black stain of blood that has begun to ooze through the cloth. Slowly he rises to his feet, and once again he hears a noise in the silence. He casts his eyes around, but the tent is full of shadows. Only the coal stove throws off a small glow of light in the corner. As he struggles to see through the darkness, he hears the flare of a match and turns to see Nan standing by the long wooden bar. She lights a lantern, then blows the match out and turns to face him. As she steps in front of the lantern, its flame casts an eerie glow of light around her. Her eyes are wide and dark, her skin pale in the half-light, and her unearthly beauty frightens him. He wonders whether he is dreaming, but then Nan crosses slowly over to the cage. She pauses just beside the door, the fingers of one hand resting on the bars.

'How is Queen?'

'She's past the worst of it.'

'Will she live?'

He hesitated. 'If she wants to.'

Nan looks at Queen and frowns. 'Why would she choose to die?'

'I don't know,' he says truthfully.

Nan looks around at the metal bars of the cage. 'Perhaps I shouldn't have come for you on the bridge.'

Nathan feels a lump rising in his throat. He has lost so much already that the idea of losing Queen is more than he can bear. He looks at her long feline form stretched out in the flickering light, and a thought comes to him for the first time. 'I think that Queen cannot forget what she once had,' he says slowly.

He turns back to Nan and she is staring at him through the bars of the cage, and something in her gaze embarrasses him.

'Do you want to come in?' he asks self-consciously.

She shakes her head. 'I want you to come out.'

He hesitates, glancing down at Queen lying asleep at his feet. He feels his heart driving hard in his chest, and a stinging in his eyes. He makes his way across the cage, stepping carefully round Nero's inert body. When he reaches the door, he opens it as quietly as he can so as not to rouse the sleeping lions. Once outside, he secures the door again and faces Nan. She stands only inches from him, and for the first time he sees that she is only just shorter than he.

'Nathan,' she says quietly. 'Do you want me?'

He opens his mouth as if to speak, but no sound comes forth. His eyes trace the lush line of her lips, and he is suddenly afraid. He does not trust his own desire, for he has seen what damage love can do.

Nan continues to stare at him. Her face is part in shadow, her expression dark and unyielding. Slowly she brings one hand up to her neck and begins to work the buttons on her dress. One by one, her slender fingers free each one in turn, until the dress hangs open to her hips. Inside she wears a pale cotton shift, so thin that he can see the outline of her breasts clearly beneath it. She pauses. He thinks fleetingly that he must stop her, before it is too late, and then she reaches for his hand and places it inside her dress. The feel of her warm, slender waist against his palm takes his breath away. He takes a step towards her, for now there is so very much he wants, and when he finally brings his lips to hers he is no longer capable of fear, or even thought.

Nan pulls him down on to the ground and yields completely to his touch, unfolding herself beneath him. He is suddenly, almost painfully, aware of all that he has ever lacked. She whispers his name as he undresses her, as if by doing so she bolsters his presence. Again and again he hears his name repeated in the darkness, and the rhythmic beat of it mingles with his own desire, with his own cavernous yearning. He feels the smooth hardness of her body writhe and turn beneath him. He is shocked by how thin she feels, her slender thighs clenched tightly round his own. He buries his face in the crescent of her neck and catches the faint smell of citrus, mixed with her own scent.

'Nathan,' she whispers again in the darkness, her fingers travelling across his shoulders and down the long arch of his spine. He moves his lips across her face and neck and shoulders, breathing in deeply so that the smell of her will stay with him. When he finally enters her, she clings tightly to his shoulders, her forehead pressed against his chin.

Much later she dozes off, the two of them entwined like eels. He gently disentangles himself from her arms and raises himself up on one elbow. Perhaps this is what Riza meant, he thinks, for he feels stricken by desire. The lantern on the bar continues to cast a flickering arc of light across the tent, and as he turns round in the half-darkness to survey the cages, he sees Queen staring at him silently, her enormous, tawny gaze unblinking. He feels a sudden pang of disloyalty. She continues to stare, and then lowers herself to the ground and closes her eyes.

Some hours later, Nathan wakes. He lies unmoving as the feeble dawn light gathers in the tent. After a time, Nan begins to stir beside him. She opens her eyes and smiles at him, and he is dazzled. He thinks of that other time, when her smile nearly cost his life. He raises a finger and runs it along her lower lip.

'I wanted to kiss you that first night,' he murmurs. 'In the cage.'

'Why didn't you?' she asks.

'I didn't dare,' he says. The image of his mother comes to him. 'I have never understood women.' Nan frowns. She reaches up and brushes a lock of hair from his eyes. 'Even my own mother,' he adds. 'Perhaps especially her . . .' His voice tails off.

'Where is she now?' Nan asks.

Nathan hesitates. The image of his mother as a young woman comes into his head. 'She's dead,' he says. 'She died a long time ago.'

Nan reaches for him, pulls him to her tightly, and wraps her body round him like a blanket. He feels a stirring and, for a split second, his mind is torn between the need for comfort and that other, aching need. Then he feels her legs part for him, and he moves quickly between them. His mind empties. He presses forward into her, pushes his muscled body as hard as he can against hers, and then, even before he realises it, he is sobbing in her arms. She stops his angry thrusting with her voice and her embrace. He feels his body begin to quake. He shuts his eyes and tries to lose himself inside her, but can think only of what he's lost. She strokes his head and whispers to him, and though he cannot hear the words, the sound of her voice soothes him. Slowly the sobbing subsides, until there is nothing left but the deadly quiet of the tent. They lie together in the stillness for a long time, until day has broken, and the animals begin to stir.

Nathan realises they too will have to rise. He forces himself to speak. 'What made you come to me last night?'

Nan hesitates a second. 'It was Shad,' she says reluctantly. 'He followed you the other night. The night you went with Lulu.' She looks away, unable to meet his gaze. 'I suppose I had to prove that he was wrong.'

'You knew I didn't want Lulu,' he says.

She nods slowly. 'But I didn't know if you wanted me.'

Nathan smoothes her hair and pulls her head down beneath his chin, so that she will not see his expression. Once again he feels dismay at the mention of her husband, and resentful of her troubled history; but he himself is not free from the burdens of the past.

'What is it that he wants?'

Nan raises her head and looks at him. 'Me.'

'And what is it that you want?' he asks.

235

She hesitates. For the first time, he can sense her fear. 'I want to start again,' she whispers. 'With you.' Nathan sees her start to tremble. He bends and presses his lips to her brow.

'Then I shall tell him so,' he murmurs.

50

Lulu

LULU STARES AT his reflection in the mirror of his dressing room. Something in his face has altered. It is as if his skin has shed a layer, and what has been exposed is somehow both raw and ravaged. He cannot transform this new self with paint and powder, for the more he applies the less it seems to conceal. He toys with the notion of removing it all: not just the make-up, but the hairpiece, the satin bustier and the sequins as well – the way he did years ago, at his father's insistence. But he cannot. He is no longer certain which part of him is true and which is false.

It has been three days since his night with Nathan, and in the intervening hours he has descended into darkness. Again and again he curses himself for upsetting the balance of his life, for now he finds himself unable to regain it. Yesterday he did not leave his room. It was Monday, the day the circus does not open, a day he normally looks forward to. Upon waking, he found himself unable to move.

He hears a scrabbling at the door of his dressing room. He turns with relief, half expecting to see Nan. Instead there is a stranger. The man is short and dark-haired with a neatly trimmed moustache and a beard that almost hides the pocks upon his face. He is perhaps ten years older than Lulu, and wears a cheap coat and a dark green tartan cap. The man glances over his shoulder, then steps inside and pulls the door closed behind him. He nods to Lulu, his dark eyes intent.

Instantly Lulu is on his guard. He squares his shoulders.

'Who are you?' he demands.

The man offers him a hand. 'I'm your biggest fan,' he says, the corners of his mouth forming the ghost of a smile.

Lulu ignores the hand. He knows only too well the scent of an admirer, and this man does not have it. 'Get out.'

The man holds up his hands in protest. 'Not so fast,' he says. 'I've only just arrived.' He looks around the tiny room, taking in the make-up jars, wigs, and costumes festooned about the walls. 'So this is it,' he says, indicating the costumes around him with raised eyebrows. 'This is Lulu.'

'I am Lulu,' he says angrily. 'But I don't know who you are. Or what you want.'

The man narrows his gaze. 'I want a story. Your story. Lulu.' This last word is uttered quietly, with the force of a punch.

Lulu looks beyond the man to the closed door of the commode, and wonders whether he should shout. Then he turns back to the mirror and reaches for a hairbrush. 'There is no story,' he says in a clipped voice, pulling the brush through his long golden hair.

The man watches him. 'The tamer has a story,' he says evenly.

Lulu stops brushing. The colour drains from his face. He stares at the man's reflection in the mirror.

'Perhaps you'd care to tell me yours.' The reporter smirks at him and takes a notepad from his pocket.

Lulu takes a deep breath, then continues brushing. 'I have no idea why you've come.'

'Don't you?' says the man. He takes a step closer and his voice drops to a hush. 'People tell us things, you know. All sorts of people. I don't know why, but they do. Sometimes it's for money. Sometimes it's for fame. Sometimes it's for spite. Anyway, it happens all the time. The lad who came to me, he didn't want my money. And he certainly wasn't looking to be famous. He just wanted me to print the truth.' The reporter grins menacingly for a moment. 'I have enough to write a story, with or without your help. Enough, perhaps, to land you both in prison,' he adds, his voice hardening.

Lulu stares at him. Nathan, at least, has not betrayed him. He is bolstered by this thought. He lays the brush down on the table and rises to his feet.

'Get out,' he says quietly. 'Before I have you thrown to the lions.'

The reporter smiles, and Lulu can see the stain of tobacco upon his teeth. 'It would make a cracking story,' says the man. 'But I'd not live to see the fee.' With that he doffs his hat in mock respect, and disappears out the door, leaving Lulu frozen behind him.

A moment later, Lulu hears a gentle knock. He stares at the door with enmity. The sound comes again, and he leans across and opens the door to find Nan standing there.

'Are you all right?'

'Why should I not be?'

'Who was that man?' She steps inside and eases the door closed behind her. Lulu looks again at the mirror. He is suddenly weary of his own reflection.

'A reporter,' he says dully.

'What did he want?'

'A revelation. He wanted to unmask my secrets.'

'You didn't speak to him.'

'I didn't need to. He knew a great deal already.'

Nan takes a deep breath and lets it out slowly. 'Oh, Lulu. I'm so sorry.'

Lulu shrugs. 'Perhaps it's for the best. My life is not so very good at the moment. Perhaps it's time for a change of scenery. Another tour abroad, perhaps . . .' His voice tails off. The thought sickens him.

Nan hesitates. 'Will he write a story?'

Lulu gives a feeble smile. 'We shall have to wait and see.'

51

Nan

WHEN NAN LEAVES Lulu, she goes in search of Nathan, but cannot find him. This morning, at his own insistence, Nathan had gone to see Shad. Relieved, Nan felt as if for once the burden of Shad was being lifted from her shoulders, and pleased at Nathan's willingness to face him on her behalf.

Now she wonders what on earth possessed her. The thought of Nathan face to face with Shad fills her with alarm. As the day drags on, her mind conjures possibilities. She does not fear for Nathan's safety, for she knows that Shad is incapable of outright violence. It is his ability to thwart her life that worries her. Nathan would not understand the depth of Shad's guile, mainly because he himself is free of it. Perhaps that is why she wants him. There is something innocent about the cage boy that she longs to bind herself to, so that she will no longer be tainted by her life.

The menagerie is empty when she enters, but already an air of normality has been restored. She crosses to the lion cage and rests her hands upon the bars. At once Nero sits up and gives an enthusiastic snarl of greeting, which pleases her. She speaks to him softly, murmurs quiet words of reassurance so as not to disturb Queen, who lies resting in the far corner. Queen already seems improved since yesterday. Nan sees with relief that she has not disturbed the dressing on her tail, and when Queen opens one eye in Nan's direction it is bright again. Nero stretches and ambles round the cage, passing within several inches of Queen's sleeping form. Nan believes it is a good sign, the two of them in proximity again.

Talliot enters with the old woman in her chair, and Nan suddenly feels conspicuous. She steps backwards from the cage. They watch her suspiciously.

'What are you doing?' asks Talliot.

'I was looking for Nathan,' she stammers. Too late, she realises she should not have used his Christian name. The old woman raises an eyebrow.

'He is gone,' she says curtly.

Nan is confused by her response. 'Where?'

'Back where he came from,' says the old woman. She wheels herself closer to the cage and stares at Queen. 'He is a stubborn boy.'

Nan sees the old woman's head tremble slightly. She glances over at Talliot, who averts his eyes. For the first time, she feels the full weight of the old woman's scrutiny.

'What is he to you?' she demands.

Nan is unable to speak, pierced like an insect by the old woman's gaze. Truthfully, she does not know the answer.

'You are better off without him,' says the old woman.

'How do you know?' she asks, suddenly seized with fear.

'Oh, I know,' says the old woman. She turns her eyes back to the lions. 'My husband was the same. I gave up everything for him. But he was like a man possessed. The lions owned him in the end.' She shakes her head slowly. 'I don't know how, but they are very much alike. Even though there's not an ounce of blood between them. He shares nothing with me.'

Nan frowns. 'Who are you?' she says.

The old woman turns back to face her. 'Did he not tell you? Nathan is my son.'

Nan stares at her, incredulous. 'He told me you were dead,' she says finally.

The old woman throws back her head and laughs. It is a joyless sound, one that makes Nan's hair stand on end. Then she falls silent, and her unsteady gaze comes to rest on the floor at her feet. Talliot clears his throat and places his hands upon the back of the wheelchair.

'We should go,' he says gently. The old woman slowly raises her head, and then her eyes seem to focus, and she nods. He begins to turn her towards the door.

'Nathan isn't gone,' Nan blurts out. They both turn to look at her.

'Then where is he?' says Talliot after a moment.

She cannot tell the truth. 'I don't know,' she says finally.

They both stare at her in silence. The old woman turns and looks at Talliot.

'And what of them?' she asks, nodding at the lions. 'Who will take the show this evening?'

Talliot shrugs. 'We'll have to cancel it.'

They hear a noise along the passage and turn to see Lulu enter through the doorway, already in full costume.

'What's wrong?' he asks, seeing their faces.

'Nathan isn't back yet,' murmurs Nan.

Lulu considers this. 'If he does not return, I will do it.'

'Lulu,' murmurs Nan, shaking her head doubtfully.

Lulu raises a hand to stay her objections. 'I could feed them,' he continues, 'the way Nathan did that first night. It cannot be so very difficult.' He looks from Nan to Talliot.

Nan frowns. Something in his manner unsettles her, for his tone is strangely offhand, and his cheeks have taken on a feverish hue.

Talliot hesitates. 'I don't think so,' he says.

'Why not? It would amuse me,' says Lulu evenly. 'Besides, the house will be full this evening. You would not disappoint the audience.'

'Let him do it, if he wishes,' says the old woman. 'He'll not come to any harm if he just feeds them. You can back him up with a pistol.'

Talliot considers this for a moment, then shrugs in acquiescence. 'All right,' he says. 'As you wish.'

Again they start to leave, when Nan interrupts them. 'Nathan will be here,' she says fervently. They turn to look at her. 'I know he will.'

52

Nathan

NATHAN STANDS OUTSIDE the house in Rotherhithe. The area is new to him, but the narrow street is like a thousand others. With its neat row of small brick cottages, he could be anywhere in London. The door opens, and Nathan recognises Shad at once.

Shad, however, is clearly taken aback. 'It's you,' he says.

'I've come to talk about Nan.'

Shad hesitates, then opens the door wide. Nathan steps inside and looks about the cluttered room with awe. He has never seen anything like it. As a child he was taken once to a museum of curiosities, where he was frightened by the strange array of mechanical displays. He feels equally uneasy now, surrounded by the shiny ornaments that fill the tiny room. He reaches up and fingers a small tin monkey hanging by the doorway, pulling a string at its base. The monkey's arms swing upwards, and at the same time, its jaws open to reveal a pearly grin. He hears Shad's voice behind him.

'First the flyer, now my Nan. Which is it to be, tamer? You can't have it both ways.'

Nathan feels himself flush. He turns to face Shad, his heart racing. 'She wants a divorce.'

Shad stares at him a moment, then bursts into laughter. 'Well, that's rich,' he says. ''Cause we were never married.'

Nathan frowns. 'But . . . there was a child,' he says slowly.

Shad nods. 'That's right. He was mine. A bastard child,' he adds pointedly. 'Didn't she say?'

Nathan shakes his head.

'He died almost straight away. She as near as killed him, Nan did. She wasn't fit to raise a child on this earth. But I don't suppose she told you that, either.'

'What do you mean?'

Shad shrugs. 'My son might have lived if it hadn't been for Nan.'

'I don't believe you.'

'Don't you? Well, maybe you should ask her. Ask Nan how she killed her baby boy.'

Nathan feels his mouth go dry. He hears a sudden ringing in his ears, as if his head is trying to shut out Shad's words. He looks again at the monkey.

Shad rocks forward on his feet. 'She's a lot like her mam, Nan is. Like both our mams. The only thing they could look to was the drink. Did she tell you about Fleur? I had a baby sister once. My mam killed her when she could barely walk. And herself. It was an accident, they said. But Nan and I knew better.' Shad waits for Nathan to speak. When he doesn't, Shad takes a step closer to him.

'I guess me and Nan were the lucky ones. We survived.

246

Our mams left us to each other. Left us together from the very start. It was almost like we were bred to be together.'

Shad's eyes are glazed with excitement, as if he is strangely elated by the tale he is telling. Nathan sees his chest rise and fall with emotion. They hear someone at the door, and both turn to see the old woman enter, her arms laden with shopping. She pauses just inside the door, wheezing heavily, then raises her head to peer at them.

'Who've we got now, Shad. More family?'

Shad hesitates a split second. 'A friend,' he says coldly.

The old woman turns to Nathan. 'You'll stay for tea I hope. We don't often have guests, Shad and me. Except for his sister.'

'Thank you, no,' Nathan murmurs.

'Shad, tell your friend he's welcome,' she continues, ignoring his words. She bends down, reaching into her bag of shopping. 'We've got smoked gammon. And fine new russet potatoes.'

'Thank you, I won't,' says Nathan a little more forcefully. He is suddenly desperate to be rid of them, and moves a step towards the door. The old woman straightens up.

'No need for haste,' she says slowly.

Nathan looks from her to Shad, who stands watching him with a smile. The room is suddenly oppressive. Nathan does not want to remain there another second. 'I'm sorry. I must be off,' he stammers. He slips past her and out of the door, leaving the tin monkey swaying behind him.

53

The Lions

NERO AND QUEEN are finally alone. The others have left the menagerie, after a seemingly endless round of muttering and argument. Nero is relieved that they are gone, especially the old woman, who makes him uneasy. Once again the cage boy is strangely absent. The rumbling in Nero's stomach tells him food is overdue.

Queen lies in the corner of the cage, making little effort to move other than to shift occasionally from one side to the other. The scent of blood still clings to Nero's nostrils. He cannot banish it, though he can see that she is no longer on the edge of death. He eyes the bandaged stump of her tail suspiciously, as if it is an enemy he cannot trust. The stump threatens their pairing, and reminds him that life within the cage has changed. In the space of a few nights, Queen has altered. She lies unmoving but does not sleep. He can hear the harsh staccato of her breath, can feel the tremor of agitation just beneath her flesh. Much of the time her eyes are open wide, although when he cuts across her line of vision she does not acknowledge him, or even focus on his form. Her luminous gaze is fixed on some place he cannot reach.

Nero is losing Queen. She may already be lost. He stares out across the tent towards Kezia's cage, but the orang-utan remains hidden in her box. Everything about the cage repels him: the sight of Queen and her suppurating wound, the pungent reek of Kezia's decline, the acrid taste of coal dust in his mouth, the punishing absence of sunlight. He craves the harsh scratch of grass against his underside, and the stinging pelt of rain upon his back, and the terrible sight of lightning on the horizon. He roars out his discontent to the semi-darkness. Again and again his anguished roars split the silence of the empty tent, until his throat is parched and sore.

Finally he collapses, panting, on to his belly. Queen has shifted her position so that her spine curls away from him. He feels the rumbling again and surrenders himself to it. Whatever else happens, Nero can always count on hunger. It comes to him like an old friend, and he finds its presence comforting. He stretches out his muscled legs in front of him, glancing for the hundredth time towards the doorway of the tent.

54
Lulu

LULU WAITS WITH knees pressed together for his cue. He is primed for performance: his hair and make-up are picture-perfect, and the sequins of his padded bustier shimmer like diamonds in the mirror of his commode. The flush of excitement has returned once again to his cheeks, and from time to time he can hear a burst of approval from the crowd, which meshes neatly with the rhythmic surging in his chest. On the dressing table in front of him lies Nathan's whip, and in his mind's eye he is already in the ring, feeling the weight of the whip in his hand and the hot stench of Nero's breath upon his face.

He hears the last act finish and rises to his feet, wetting his lips in the mirror, and tucking a stray wisp of blond hair back into his tiara. He pulls on elbow-length white gloves and reaches for the whip. Its neat round handle sits nicely in his grip, and he gives a short flick of his wrist. The thick leather thong leaps across his tiny dressing room like a snake, and Lulu breathes in sharply at the sight. He slips the handle of the whip into the waist of his satin bloomers and makes his way to the ring. He has already performed once this evening, flying high overhead. Now it is time for Nero.

Lulu fizzes with adrenalin as he approaches the ring. He has courted danger since he was old enough to walk. Without it he would perish. It defines him in some uneasy way, gives substance and shape to his life, both in and out of the ring. To seek the love of other men is the greatest risk of all; Lulu knows this know. It is the most daredevil feat in his vast array of stunts and, sooner or later, it will mean his undoing.

As he strides towards the ring, Talliot steps out from nowhere and lays a hand on his arm. The older man's face is tight with disapproval, and Lulu can see the strain of it upon his features.

Lulu smiles reassuringly. 'Don't worry,' he says quickly, just as Talliot opens his mouth to speak.

Talliot tightens his grip on Lulu's forearm. 'You've got five minutes,' he says tersely. 'Just feed him. Nothing more. Do you understand?'

Lulu smiles artfully; after all, he is an entertainer.

'I'll be right here,' says Talliot, patting his side.

Lulu glances down to see the bulge of a revolver concealed beneath his waistcoat. He raises his eyes to Talliot. 'Nero is waiting,' he says, and after a moment's hesitation, Talliot releases his arm. Lulu picks up the metal bucket of butchered horsemeat that lies at Talliot's feet and enters the oval cage. At once Nero rises to all fours and looks him squarely in the eye. Lulu blanches. He has never been this close to Nero, and he is startled by the lion's enormous bulk. Nero's tail lashes cautiously from side to side, and his large black nostrils tremble with anticipation. He gives an irritated shake of his great, shaggy head, and Lulu stares at him, transfixed. For the first time ever he is not alone in the ring. He cannot predict the outcome, and neither can he control it. The thought thrills him. He remembers the crowd suddenly, and raises a gloved hand to wave, never once taking his eyes from the lion. The crowd responds with an enthusiastic cheer.

Nero gives several sharp snarls in a row, then takes a few steps backwards, nervously. Lulu raises the whip and cracks it overhead. He is surprised by its lightness, and the noise of it excites him. He smiles broadly, and motions towards the nearest pedestal as he has seen Nathan do, barking out a command. Nero hesitates, then leaps up on to the pedestal and seats himself a little awkwardly. He gives a sharp snarl of assent, and in response Lulu reaches in the bucket and pulls forth a fist-sized chunk of gristled meat. He throws it right at Nero and the lion's jaws snap closed on it with murderous speed. He swallows the lump instantly, then roars with agitation, his angry eyes flashing to the bucket at Lulu's feet.

You must work for it, thinks Lulu, just as we all do. The audience claps with approval, and from the wings Lulu hears Talliot hiss his name angrily. Lulu ignores Talliot. Instead he locks his gaze on Nero's. The lion's eyes seem to swell and change colour. Lulu cracks the whip again and Nero snarls in response. Lulu sees the sudden swell of Nero's muscles, sees the hair upon the lion's neck stand on end. He has a sudden urge to make the lion fly. He motions to the next pedestal and calls out a command, and as soon as Nero lands, Lulu cracks the whip and orders him to leap again. Nero hesitates a moment, then leaps to the next pedestal, and Lulu begins to bark out commands in rapid succession, cracking the whip every few seconds, urging Nero on from pedestal to pedestal.

The sight of the massive animal bounding around exhilarates him. He feels an enormous rush of excitement, perhaps the greatest thrill he's ever known. He raises his voice so the lion can hear his commands above the roar of the crowd, so that he can blot out the angry calls of Talliot in the distance, and so that he can forget himself. Lulu shouts repeatedly at the bewildered lion, who stops all of a sudden and turns on him. His open jaws are lathered with rage. The crowd erupts with excitement, and Lulu hears a woman shriek in the audience. He turns his head to the crowd. And then it happens all at once: the hammering blow of Nero's feet against his chest, the searing pain in his neck, the flash of light behind his eyes, and the blast of gunfire in his ears.

Lulu's final thought, before darkness overtakes him, is of relief.

55
Nan

IT TAKES TWO shots to silence Nero. The first strikes him on the shoulder, throwing him sideways to the floor. Nero struggles to his feet, his expression one of complete confusion. The second catches him behind the ear and fells him for good. Nan rushes forward from her place in the aisle and stops just inches from the cage. Lulu lies unmoving on the floor of the ring, blood flowing freely from a wound in his neck. Talliot and the others run into the cage, and Nan watches as they try to staunch the flow of blood with their clothing. For once, the crowd is eerily silent. After a few moments, a woman quietly begins to weep.

Nan stares across the ring to Lulu's ashen face. She knows with icy certainty that he has sought his own escape, and that she played a part in his undoing. For it is she who caught the hand of love, and Lulu who missed it. And now it is too late to make amends. The thought paralyses her, and it is not until Talliot takes her arm that she realises she is needed.

They take him by horse and cart to St Thomas's Hospital, a journey of less than half a mile. The ride seems endless to Nan. She crouches by Lulu's side, holding his hand as tightly as she dares. She can see the rise and fall of his chest, but cannot feel a pulse. Lulu's mouth hangs slackly open, and his neck is twisted round with bandages. Nan watches in horror as the blood slowly begins to seep through the cloth. When they arrive at the hospital, an attendant stops them at the gate. He moves Lulu from the cart to a trolley, then wheels him away, leaving Talliot and Nan to stare after his disappearing body. Talliot turns to her and lays a hand upon her arm. 'I must return,' he says apologetically.

Nan is forced to wait in a dimly lit corridor near the entrance. She has eaten nothing all day, and the clinging smell of carbolic makes her stomach lurch. After two hours, a bearded young surgeon with bloodshot eyes comes to find her. He wearily explains that Lulu is unlikely to regain consciousness that night, as he is heavily sedated, and Nan's presence might be more useful in the morning. He turns away without another word, releasing her. Nan stares dumbly down the corridor. She feels disloyal leaving. But Lulu has leaped without her, and she does not know where he has landed.

56

Nathan

I T IS PAST midnight, and Nathan stares uncertainly into the darkness of the menagerie. Inside, the tent is deathly quiet, and he pauses on the threshold, afraid suddenly to enter. He is half frozen. He has spent the evening wandering, trying to make sense of Shad's words. In the end he has come to Lambeth Walk, as if London holds no other paths for him but this one.

He feels his way to the bar and gropes along its wooden surface until he finds a lantern and a box of matches. He lights the lamp and stares down at his red and swollen fingers. In the faint, flickering glow he barely recognises them. He brings them to his mouth, but the warmth of his breath seems to evaporate instantly in the chill of the tent. He replenishes the stove with coal, then returns to the bar and reaches beneath the counter for a bottle of brandy, pouring himself a glass with shaking hands. The brandy stings his lips and brings a slow burn to his stomach.

He turns to the lion cage, and for the first time sees that

Queen is alone. She lies unmoving on her side, but he can see that she is not asleep. He looks around the tent in confusion, for there is no sign of Nero, and as he does his heart begins to race. In the far corner of the tent, behind the lion cage, Nathan's gaze finally comes to rest on a large lump of sailcloth pushed back against the wall. He eyes it for a moment, then advances slowly towards it. He crouches down on his haunches and slowly peels back a corner of the canvas, almost certain now of what lies beneath.

Nevertheless, he is still struck dumb by the sight. Nero's massive form has already been diminished by death. His tawny eyes have turned to grey, and his magnificent mane is matted with blood. His mouth hangs open unnaturally, forming a strangled sort of yawn, and his legs lie at odd angles, like sticks of timber hurriedly thrown in a heap. Even his head seems smaller, as if death had drained it.

Nathan hastily pulls the cover over Nero's carcass, for it is not an image he would like to carry with him. He glances back at Queen. If she is aware of Nero's death, she gives no indication. She lies still, as if in a trance. He moves towards her. What he wants, more than anything, is a sign from Queen to show that she has not forgotten their bond. He circles round to the front of the cage and unlocks it, approaching her slowly, murmuring words of encouragement. As he does, Queen raises her head and swivels round to face him. She blinks several times, staring right at him, and in that instant Nathan feels himself fade and disappear. Queen sees nothing, and Nathan knows that he has lost them both.

He returns to the bar and picks up his drink. As he does, he hears a noise and turns to see Nan in the doorway, clutching Lulu's olive frock coat.

'Nathan,' she murmurs, taking a few steps forward. She looks both anguished and afraid.

'Nero is dead,' he says, his voice cracking slightly in the stillness.

'He nearly killed Lulu,' she says. 'Talliot had to shoot him.'

Nathan frowns. 'Where is Lulu?'

'In the hospital.' She pauses. 'He'll be lucky to survive, Nathan.'

Nathan feels his heart sink. He stares down at the tumbler of brandy, and the glass nearly swims before his eyes. 'I should have returned earlier,' he whispers.

'Where were you?'

Nathan looks at her but does not speak. Eventually she answers for him. 'You found Shad.'

Nathan nods.

Nan takes a step forward. 'Nathan, you must tell me.'

He looks down at his glass, for he cannot meet her gaze. 'He said that you weren't fit to raise a child, Nan. He said that you as near as killed him . . .' His voice tails off guiltily.

Nan shakes her head. 'It wasn't like that.'

Nathan looks at her uncertainly. She comes towards him.

'Nathan, you must believe me. Shad would say anything to get me back.'

'He said the baby would have survived if you had listened to him.'

Nan takes a deep breath and exhales. 'Shad thought the baby didn't stand a chance with us in the rookery. He wanted me to give it to a home. He was terrified, Nathan. He didn't want to see the baby die. But I couldn't do it. Not for anything. I couldn't give my baby away.'

She pauses for a moment and sighs. 'I don't know if my son died because we were poor or just unlucky. Or because Shad and I weren't meant to be together.' Her voice drops. 'But I loved my son more than anything in the world, Nathan. And when he died, I wanted to die with him.'

'He said that you were bred to be together. Why didn't you tell me about him, Nan? About the two of you?'

She shakes her head. 'How could I? Shad isn't like other people, Nathan. He lives in his own world.' She sighs. 'I thought that if you spoke to him, that if you saw how he was, then maybe you'd understand . . .' Her voice tails off. She looks down glumly, picks at the thread of her skirt. 'Nathan, I feel as if my whole life has been about Shad. I don't want it to be about him any longer.'

Nathan looks at her, thinking of the life that has dogged them both. Then his mind flies to the long grass and open skies of the prairie. The idea of it is like a prayer. 'We must leave,' he says.

57

Queen

QUEEN LIES UNMOVING in her cage. The cage boy has gone, but she is past caring. She knows as well that Nero is dead, for she watched as four strong men dragged his body back to the menagerie earlier this evening. She felt nothing at the time. His bloodied carcass seemed little more than freshly killed meat.

Now, for the first time since her capture, Queen is alone. She stares out into the darkness without purpose, for she seeks nothing. Thankfully, her yearning has ceased. She feels calm, light-headed, not quite of this place. She hears a scrambling just outside the doorway of the tent, the sound of feet stumbling in the dark, and a man coughing. And then a strange scent reaches her nostrils, a slightly sweet, sharpish odour that rolls across the floor of the menagerie to where she lies. She rises to her feet, crosses over to the bars, and waits. Her instinct tells her that she must be ready. And when she finally sees the bright orange flame bloom like an orchid in the corner, she meets it evenly with her lion's gaze.

58

Nathan

NATHAN WAKES WITH a jolt, his heart beating hard. Beside him, Nan sleeps deeply. He eases out from under the bedclothes and quickly dresses, for he knows with perfect certainty that something is wrong. He tiptoes down the dark stairwell and opens the front door, slipping noiselessly out into the street. There is a strong breeze and the clouds scuttle by quickly. He does not know how long they have slept, for it was after one o'clock when he and Nan returned to his room. But now the street is deathly still, and Nathan senses that dawn is not far off.

He pulls his coat tightly round him and heads for Lambeth Walk. It is only five minutes away, but as he rounds the first corner he breaks into a lope, for already he can smell the fire. Nathan jogs along the cobbled pavements, panting hard in the cold night air, and before long he can see the dull glow, like a false dawn, stretching beyond the rooftops. The smell is stronger now, and as he draws closer he begins to see the smoke. It billows out in great gusts, carried along by the night wind. Nathan rounds the last corner and stops short, for ahead of him is an inferno. Both the main tent and the menagerie are ablaze, and the fire has leaped across the short yard to the roof of the houses beyond. The sight is both magnificent and terrifying. For a split second he is too stunned to think. Then he remembers Queen and the others. The menagerie is like an enormous pyre, with amber flames leaping thirty yards up into the sky. The canvas has been burned away, and the massive iron girders that held up the tent have begun to glow bright red. Nathan searches desperately in the conflagration below, but all that remains is a mass of rubble and flame.

He is not alone, for half a dozen others have also arrived to stare open-mouthed at the blaze. Water, he thinks desperately, but the vast column of fire already dwarfs them. Nathan hears a noise and turns to see two fire engines appear at the opposite end of the street. Each is drawn by a pair of dappled grey horses, eyes rolled back, nostrils flared, hoofs crashing on the cobblestones. The horses gallop flat out and the second engine nearly overturns as it takes the bend too sharply. The horses skid to a halt, and the dark-coated firemen jump down and set about unfurling hoses and unloading ladders.

Nathan watches in numb silence, feeling powerless. Then he sees the small wooden shed where the horses are stabled, not ten yards from the menagerie. By some miracle of nature, the stable is not yet alight. As he watches, a dart of flame skips across the void and in the next instant the stable roof is burning.

Nathan races to the stable and throws open the door. He

can hear the horses thrash and neigh inside their stalls. He searches in the darkness for an old blanket, and uses his teeth to tear off two long strips of wool. He unlatches the door to the first stall and opens it to reveal the terrified animal inside. He freezes; he has always hated horses. As he steps forward and reaches out a hand, there is an explosion outside. The horse rears up on its hind legs and Nathan flattens himself against the wall. Flames shoot through the ceiling and he lunges, grabbing the horse by its mane and pulling with all his might. With his free hand he wraps one of the woollen strips around the horse's eyes, and immediately the animal calms. Quickly he leads the horse out of the stall to the entrance of the stable, where he ties it firmly to the door. He runs back inside and moments later he is leading both blindfolded horses out on to the street, firemen rushing all around him. He ties the horses to a lamppost and races back to the fire.

In the space of those few minutes the flames have engulfed one of the houses and are spreading to the next. Rats scurry from the foundations, scampering across the yard in every direction. The firemen are busy emptying the houses of their occupants, and the street outside is now filling up with onlookers. Not twenty feet from where Nathan stands, two men struggle with crowbars to open a hydrant. They work quickly and quietly, their faces set with grim determination, and when they finally succeed Nathan sees one of them take a deep breath. They attach a canvas well to the hydrant, which fills like a cistern with water, and three hoses are thrust into the cavity. The pumps begin to draw water, and when it finally gushes froth from the nozzle the firemen aim right at the flames.

The two circus tents are already burned beyond salvage, so the firemen aim for the row of houses. After a split second's delay, Nathan hears a tremendous hiss of steam as the water hits the fire. He sees the firemen shrink back as a wall of heat surges at them, their arms raised to cover their faces, their skin glowing pink in the back light. The crowds are gathering now, and several policemen have arrived. Along with many others, Nathan is swept backwards in the street behind a barricade. He strains to see over the shoulders of a burly policeman in front of him as a young woman is carried screaming from a burning house. She points hysterically towards an upper floor. A moment later, two firemen scramble up a ladder, disappearing through a window behind a wall of smoke and flames. The crowd suddenly grows quiet, awaiting the outcome, and when the men emerge moments later carrying two children a wild cheer goes up around him.

Nathan cannot tear his eyes from the fire. It rages unchecked, licking up the sides of the houses, hurling across the rooftops. Dozens of people continue to pour from the row of houses, many with armloads of possessions. He peers through the bright orange glow, struggling to catch a glimpse of each face that emerges, but nowhere does he see the one that he is looking for. Nowhere does he see his mother.

59

Lulu

L ULU LIES UNCONSCIOUS in his hospital bed. He is flying high tonight, higher than he's ever been before. The crowd beneath is fading fast. Their tiny, eager, upturned faces swarm far below him. For the first time Lulu wonders why they've come, for tonight he does not need their frenzied hum. Tonight, the flight is all that matters: air and space and balance and weightlessness.

He goes through his routine and the exhilaration is divine. Suddenly he is a boy again, a boy of sixteen with another for the very first time, and Lulu almost weeps with gratitude. The boy's skin meshes with his own, his lips are Lulu's lips, his muscles arms clutch Lulu with youthful certainty. Lulu's performance is flawless tonight, the best he's ever done, and as he flies through the air he no longer needs the earth.

He prepares for his final stunt, something he's been working towards for many months, perhaps a lifetime. He sees the bar rising towards him, sees its polished wooden surface shimmer in the sparkle of the gaslight, and knows that the moment he must reach for it is near. Then, at the last second, something stays his hand. This time Lulu does not reach. Instead he flies through the air in a freefall, and the rush is almost more than he can bear. The crowd below has disappeared entirely now, and still Lulu flies through space and time, as if he were an angel.

On and on he flies, straight into his mother's arms.

60
Nan

N AN DOES NOT wake until mid-morning, and her first thought upon seeing the empty space beside her is one of alarm. Then she remembers Nathan's whispered words of reassurance in the night. Perhaps he has gone to tend Queen, she thinks. She dresses quickly, hoping she will not meet his landlady, and is relieved to find the house deserted when she slips down the stairs.

Once outside, she smells the fire almost at once, though the weather is wet and a bitter wind bites the air. Every now and then a cloud of black smoke appears above the house-tops, and the air is littered with tiny flakes of carbon, which skip along the rooftops. Like Nathan, she goes directly to Talliot's. When she reaches Lambeth Walk, she is confronted by a wall of onlookers. She strains to see past them, but all that remains of the circus is a mound of blackened rubble. Nan stares with shock at the space where the menagerie had been. She can see that the worst is past, for though several buildings have been destroyed, those surrounding them are not alight. The ground is wet from rain, and the charred remains of the burned buildings still smoulder. Every now and then a flame leaps up out of nowhere, and the tired-looking firemen attack it with their hoses. Nan stares at the destruction and, as she does so, an image from her childhood slowly comes to mind: Shad stands in the alley just behind their house, waving burning rags like a banner. Her insides tighten.

Desperately, she begins to search the crowd for Nathan. It takes her several minutes to find him, for by this time the fire has drawn several hundred onlookers, who mill about the surrounding streets with the air of revellers at a country fair. Already a handful of enterprising hawkers have set up stalls selling hot drinks and food, and even the firemen stand around in clutches of three and four, taking swigs of brandy from a bottle.

She finally locates him just behind the barricade, wet through and half frozen. His face is black with soot, and even his eyelids and nostrils are smudged with ash. 'Nathan,' she says, taking his arm and turning him towards her, away from the fire. He folds right into her without a word, his body shaking with exhaustion. He seems relieved when she leads him through the crowded streets back to his room. Once there she strips off all his clothes and puts him to bed, covering him with everything she can find: blankets, coats, clothes, even an old rug from the floor. She wipes his face with a moistened cloth, and when she is satisfied that she has removed every residue of the fire, she goes downstairs in search of something hot for him to eat.

This time Nan is not afraid when she comes face to face with his landlady at the entrance to the kitchen. 'Who are you?' the old woman demands in a tone of alarm. She is perhaps fifty, and the fleshy paunch of her cheeks is crisscrossed with tiny lines.

'I'm Nathan's wife,' Nan says evenly. The old woman looks her up and down, her eyes narrowing, then grudgingly stands aside for her to pass. Nan bites back a smile. It is not so hard a thing to find a husband, she thinks, as she sets about making tea and toast like any housewife. When she returns to his room, Nathan consumes it without a word. She lies next to him upon the bed, smoothes his brow with her long, cool fingers, until he falls deeply into sleep.

Only then does she rise and make her way to the hospital, for the spectre of Lulu has been with her all this time. She goes directly to the ward where she left him, but the moment she utters his name to the nursing sister in charge, she knows from the woman's expression that he is dead.

'His death was quiet,' the nurse says in a practised tone. Nan stares at her with enmity for nothing could be further from the truth.

'May I see him?' she asks.

The nurse looks at her strangely, before shaking her head. 'I'm sorry,' she replies. 'But the dead do not remain on the wards.'

'Yes, of course,' Nan murmurs.

'Are you the next of kin?' the sister asks.

Nan looks at her. 'Yes,' she says, for if not her, then who? She thinks of the night when they first met: how Lulu appeared before her in the street like an angel of grace, and led her safely back into the land of the living.

The nurse asks her to wait on a wooden bench at the entrance to the draughty hall, and after a few minutes someone hands her a lukewarm cup of tea. Still later there are papers to sign, and finally, a tightly wrapped bundle of Lulu's clothes is placed in her arms. As she hurries from the hospital, Nan cradles the bundle to her chest as if it were her child.

61

Nathan

THE FOLLOWING MORNING, Nathan stands amidst the charred remains of his former life. The crowds have gone, though every few minutes a few stragglers appear to gaze and point at the sight. Nathan picks his way through the rubble. The steel cages were melted in the fire, and every now and then he comes upon a tangled mass of blackened bars. Nathan kicks them with his feet, and they flake at his touch. However, no evidence of the animals remains. He does not know what he hoped to find; if some vestige of Queen and the others had survived, he would not wish to come upon it in this way. Still he searches for them in vain.

He feels someone behind him and turns to see the Skeleton Man standing quietly on the street beyond. He gives a small, rueful smile, then advances slowly to where Nathan stands in the centre. When he reaches him, the Skeleton Man stretches out a bony hand to his shoulder. At the feel of it, a lump rises in Nathan's throat.

'I'm sorry,' the Skeleton Man says. He looks down at the charred tangle of iron bars at his feet. 'Perhaps it's for the best, Nathan. Life in a cage is one that few of us would choose.' He drops his arm and looks around him. 'Fire is a great leveller,' he says. He prods a blackened lump with his toe and it dissolves into ash. 'Air, carbon, water. At the end of the day, this is all we consist of. Nothing more.'

Nathan thinks of the man's family. 'What will you do now?'

The Skeleton Man shrugs. 'What I have always done,' he says. 'Survive. By any means necessary.'

Nathan smiles. Not for the first time, the man in front of him reminds him of Riza. 'I wish you well,' he says.

The Skeleton Man extends a bony hand. Nathan clasps it in his own. The hand is surprisingly soft, warm and fragile, like the body of a bird.

'God bless you,' says the Skeleton Man.

Nathan watches him slowly thread his way back to the street. When he turns back to the scene of the fire, he is surprised to see Talliot emerge from one of the burned houses, accompanied by a man in a dark suit. The two men stand and confer for a moment, and then the dark-suited man tips his hat and turns to leave, walking quickly away, as if he is anxious to put the place behind him. Talliot looks across to where Nathan stands, and it takes him a moment to register his presence. But when he does, he slowly crosses the yard. Talliot's face is heavily lined from lack of sleep, and as he draws closer, Nathan sees that his breathing is laboured.

'Nathan,' he says, with a grim nod. 'I should have sent for you.'

Nathan looks at him, sees that his clothes are unkempt, his pallor almost grey. 'Are you all right?' he asks. Talliot nods, though he seems, for the moment, unable to speak. He takes a deep breath and glances at the space where the menagerie had been.

'Your mother is dead,' he says after a moment. He turns back to face Nathan. 'She . . . perished in the fire. They did not find her body for some hours, for she had locked herself into a storeroom.' He pauses, kicking uneasily at the ground. 'I do not think she intended to be found,' he says. 'Not alive, at any rate.' Talliot's voice cracks, and he blinks several times.

Nathan takes a deep breath and slowly exhales. Something shifts inside him.

'She was a remarkable woman in her time,' continues Talliot. 'Before the accident. And before her husband died. She never quite . . . regained herself somehow.' Talliot stares off into the distance, frowning at the memory.

'Were you in love with her?' Nathan asks quietly. The question has emerged from nowhere, and it startles even him.

Talliot does not answer at first, and Nathan wonders whether he has heard. Finally, he gives a little cough, faces Nathan, his expression heavy-hearted. 'Yes,' he says. 'I suppose I was.' He attempts a smile. 'Though she did not return my feelings.'

'I'm sorry,' Nathan murmurs.

'It did not matter,' continues Talliot after a moment. 'I drew strength from her presence. And solace from the fact that I could be of some comfort to her in the end. For she was very much alone, you see.' Too late, he realises the

273

implication of this last statement, and looks away guiltily. He clears his throat. 'I'm afraid I can offer nothing to justify her actions. She was not an easy person to understand. Or to love.'

The two men stand in silence. Nathan watches as a pair of dirty boys clamber out of a ground-floor window of one of the burned houses. They shriek with laughter, and disappear down the street.

'Did she ever speak of me?' he asks finally.

Talliot frowns. 'Only once. Some time ago. After he died.'

'What did she say?'

Talliot hesitates. 'She said that you were better off without her.'

Nathan stares numbly at the wreckage of the fire. He understands now that his mother could not live with him. Perhaps she could not live with herself once she had left him. He wonders whether, under different circumstances, they might have stayed together. For an instant, he is tempted by the idea of that other life, but the image fades almost as soon as it forms. He will never have an opportunity to live that life. So he must be content with his own.

62

Nathan

NATHAN STANDS TENTATIVELY in the doorway leading out on to the ship's upper deck. Beyond him, Nan is beckoning. It has taken her two days to coax him this far, for the sight of boundless water still unnerves him.

'Nathan,' she says smiling. 'It's the same.'

'No,' he says. 'The bridge is fixed. Like land.'

'But the water . . .' she persists.

He shakes his head.

She laughs then. 'All right. But it is wondrous just the same.'

'Yes,' he agrees. For he can see it now: the immense roll and swell of it, like the rhythmic pulse of some great beast. He cannot hide from the ocean any longer.

He advances on to the deck until he is standing by the rails. Perhaps it is the idea of it that bothers him most: the possibility that it will never end. Nan smiles at her small victory. The winter sky is blue this morning, and the water a very pale shade of green. Nathan stands at the railing, finally looking down on the vast ocean. In truth, he does not fear the water as he did the last time, but it is the earth he yearns for: the long brown grass and rich black soil of the plains.

He is finished with the circus. He needs a more private endeavour, for it is not in his nature to seek applause. He needs to plant himself in the cool, clean earth rather than in the sullied minds of men. If he can, he intends to buy a plot of land when he returns, a parcel small enough to work himself. He would like to breed livestock: chickens, pigs, sheep, perhaps even cows.

For he is good with animals. That much he knows. For a moment, he allows himself to dwell on Queen. He still hankers for her presence: for the sheer size and weight and smell of her, for her savage bulk and warmth. He will have to live without these things. But his mother's death has eased his longing. Slowly, almost without realising, his mind has pieced together a final portrait of her, the one that will stay with him.

Nan frowns at him. 'You are troubled.'

'No,' he says gently, taking her hand, and giving it a squeeze. He must still reassure her. Nan is content to leave her old life behind, to obliterate the past with the prospect of the future. But there they differ. Nathan knows he cannot afford to break with his own history, but neither can he covet it.

He closes his eyes, leans out across the railing and takes a deep breath of the briny air. Once again Nathan flies across the ocean like an albatross, and he will not rest until his feet land upon the soil of his birth.

Acknowledgements

For their comments and assistance, I am very grateful to Charlotte Mendelson, Ros Ellis, Felicity Rubinstein, Sarah Lutyens, Susannah Godman, Randal Keynes, Zelfa Hourani, Peter Sands and David Jamiesson of the Circus Friends Association of Great Britain.

As this is a work of fiction, I have taken liberties with some dates and names. However, for the factual background to the novel, the many books I found useful included: George Speaight's *A History of The Circus*, Thomas Frost's *Circus Life and Circus Celebrities*, Edwin Norwood's *The Circus Menagerie*, Tom Ogden's *Two Hundred Years of the American Circus*, Joanne Joys' *The Wild Animal Trainer in America*, Sharon Rendell's *Living With Big Cats* and Arthur Cyril Parker's *The Lion Tamers*.

On 19th Century London, Henry Mayhew's *London Labour and the London Poor*, Roy Porter's *London: A Social History*, Max Schlesinger's *Saunterings In and About London*, Kellow Chesney's *The Victorian Underworld*, Ronald Pearsall's *The Worm In The Bud: The World of Victorian Sexuality*, Francis

Russell's *London Fogs*, and Derek Hudson's *Munby: Man of Two Worlds*.

Finally, irrespective of the moral questions associated with animal training, I am indebted to all those who spent their working lives inside a cage and chose to write about it: Carl Hagenbeck, George Conklin, Clyde Beatty, Willan Bosworth, Paul Eipper, Alfred Court, Patricia Bourne, Edward Campbell, Charly Baumann and David Tetzlaff.